CHICAGOLAND DETECTIVE AGENCY

No 2

The Maltese Mummy

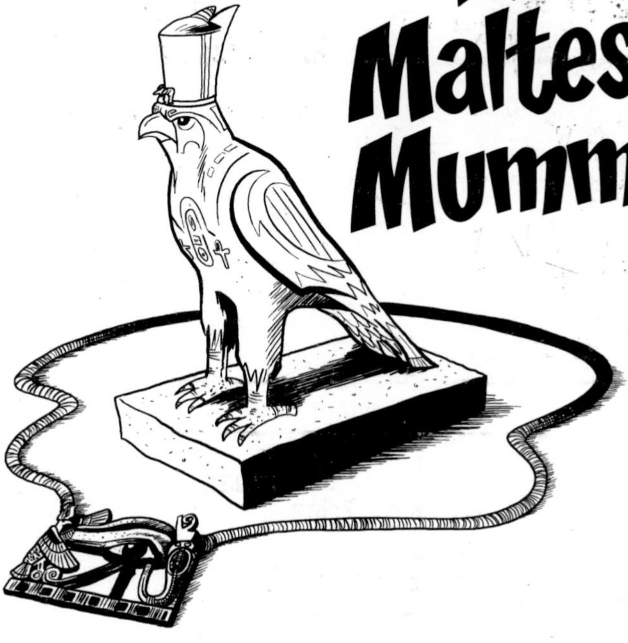

TRINA ROBBINS

ILLUSTRATED BY TYLER PAGE

GRAPHIC UNIVERSE™ • MINNEAPOLIS • NEW YORK

STORY BY **TRINA ROBBINS**

PENCILS AND INKS BY **TYLER PAGE**

LETTERING BY **ZACH GIALLONGO**

Copyright © 2011 by Lerner Publishing Group, Inc.

Graphic Universe™ is a trademark of Lerner Publishing Group, Inc.

Graphic Universe™
A division of Lerner Publishing Group, Inc.
241 First Avenue North
Minneapolis, MN 55401 U.S.A.

Website address: www.lernerbooks.com

Library of Congress Cataloging-in-Publication Data

Robbins, Trina.
      The Maltese mummy / by Trina Robbins ; illustrated by Tyler Page.
         p.   cm. — (Chicagoland Detective Agency ; #2)
      Summary: As the founders of the Chicagoland Detective Agency, a
   haiku-writing girl and a boy with a talking dog have more than enough
   cases on their hands (and paws) when a friend vanishes, a mummy's amulet
   disappears, and an evil scientist stalks human brains and hearts.
      ISBN: 978-0-7613-4615-9 (lib. bdg. : alk. paper)
      1. Graphic novels. [1. Graphic novels. 2. Mystery and detective stories.
   3. Mummies—Fiction. 4. Egypt—Antiquities—Fiction. 5. Chicago (Ill.)—
   Fiction.] I. Page, Tyler, 1976– ill. II. Title.
   PZ7.7.R632Mal 2011
   741.5'973—dc22   2010028273

Manufactured in the United States of America
1 – BC – 12/31/10

CHAPTER ONE:
ODD DOG OUT

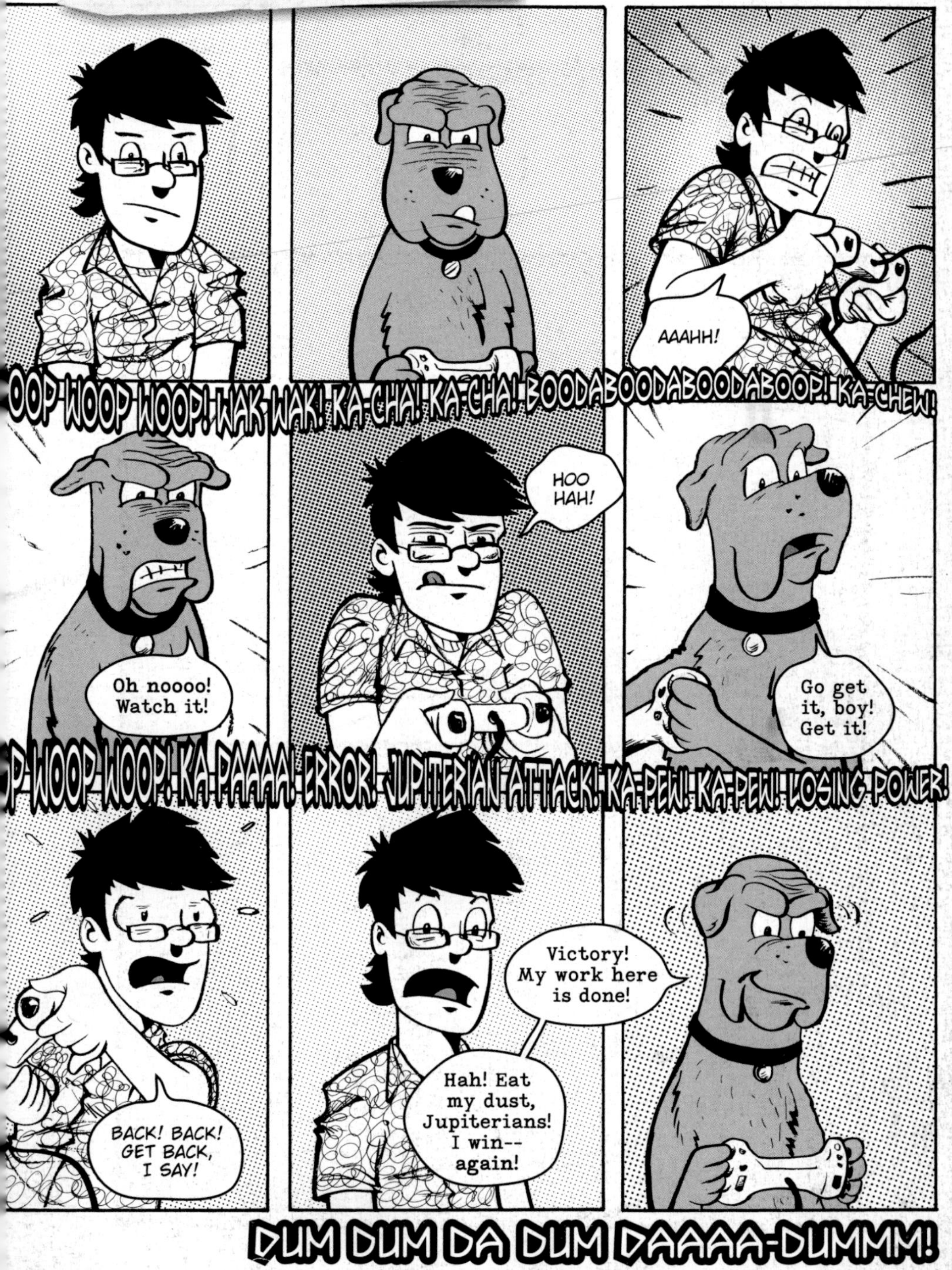
AAAHH!
OOP WOOP WOOP! WAK WAK! KA-CHA! KA-CHA! BOODABOODABOODABOOP! KA-CHEW!
Oh noooo! Watch it!
HOO HAH!
Go get it, boy! Get it!
P WOOP WOOP! KA-PAAAA! ERROR! JUPITERIAN ATTACK! KA-PEW! KA-PEW! LOSING POWER!
BACK! BACK! GET BACK, I SAY!
Hah! Eat my dust, Jupiterians! I win-- again!
Victory! My work here is done!
DUM DUM DA DUM DAAAA-DUMMM!

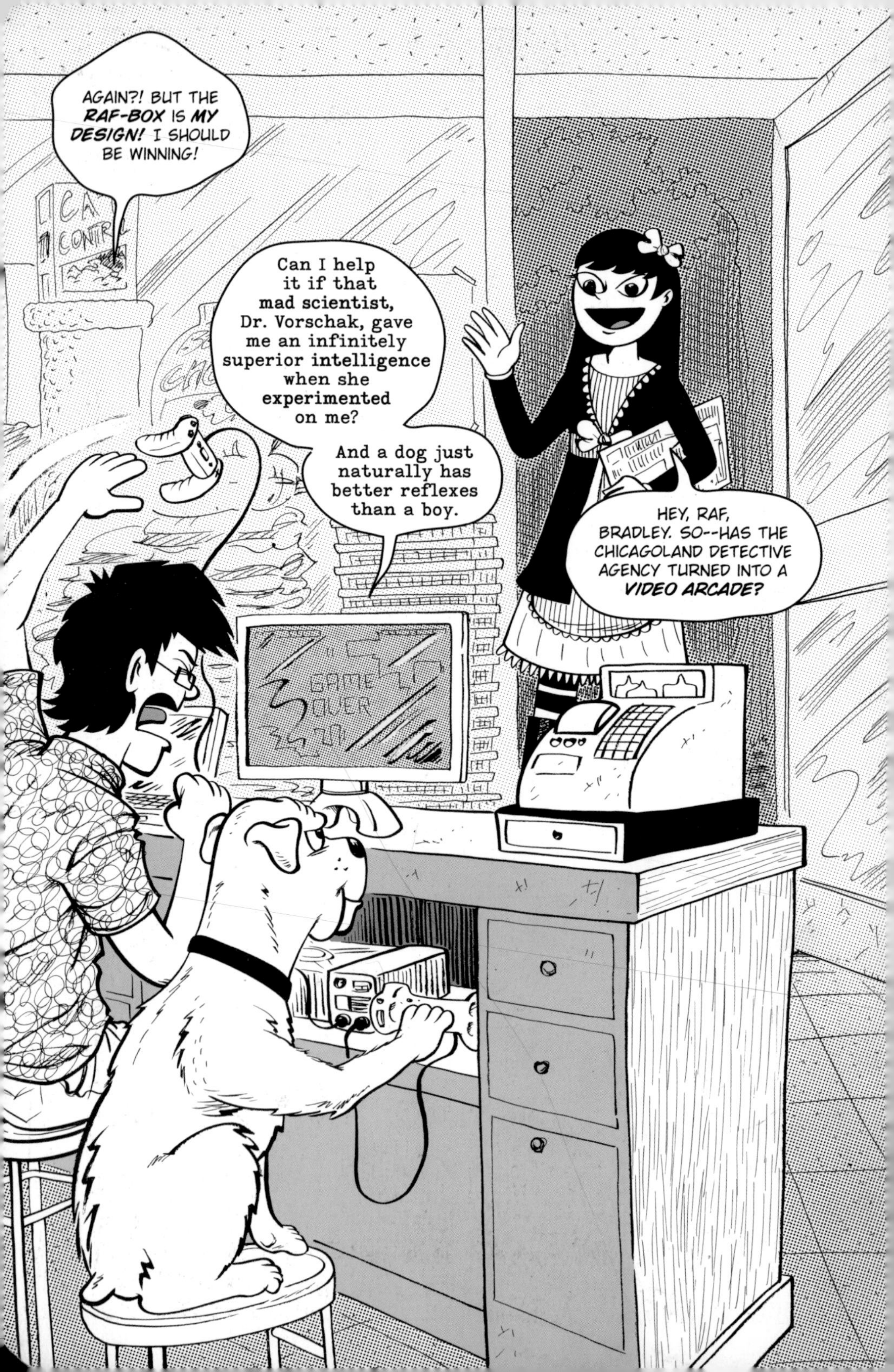
AGAIN?! BUT THE ***RAF-BOX*** IS ***MY DESIGN!*** I SHOULD BE WINNING!
Can I help it if that mad scientist, Dr. Vorschak, gave me an infinitely superior intelligence when she experimented on me?
And a dog just naturally has better reflexes than a boy.
HEY, RAF, BRADLEY. SO--HAS THE CHICAGOLAND DETECTIVE AGENCY TURNED INTO A ***VIDEO ARCADE?***
GAME OVER

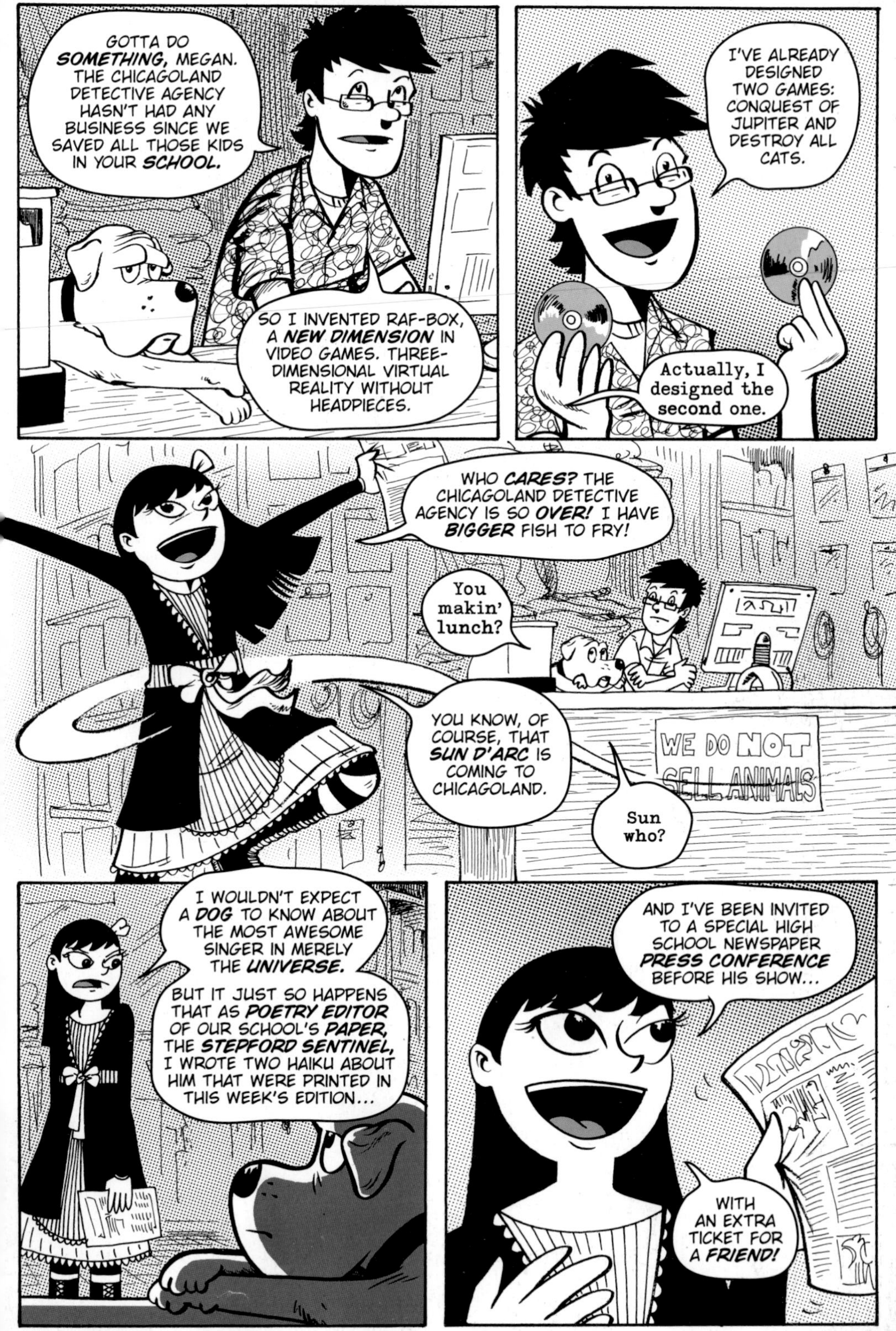
GOTTA DO SOMETHING, MEGAN. THE CHICAGOLAND DETECTIVE AGENCY HASN'T HAD ANY BUSINESS SINCE WE SAVED ALL THOSE KIDS IN YOUR SCHOOL.
SO I INVENTED RAF-BOX, A NEW DIMENSION IN VIDEO GAMES. THREE-DIMENSIONAL VIRTUAL REALITY WITHOUT HEADPIECES.
I'VE ALREADY DESIGNED TWO GAMES: CONQUEST OF JUPITER AND DESTROY ALL CATS.
Actually, I designed the second one.
WHO CARES? THE CHICAGOLAND DETECTIVE AGENCY IS SO OVER! I HAVE BIGGER FISH TO FRY!
You makin' lunch?
YOU KNOW, OF COURSE, THAT SUN D'ARC IS COMING TO CHICAGOLAND.
WE DO NOT SELL ANIMALS
Sun who?
I WOULDN'T EXPECT A DOG TO KNOW ABOUT THE MOST AWESOME SINGER IN MERELY THE UNIVERSE.
BUT IT JUST SO HAPPENS THAT AS POETRY EDITOR OF OUR SCHOOL'S PAPER, THE STEPFORD SENTINEL, I WROTE TWO HAIKU ABOUT HIM THAT WERE PRINTED IN THIS WEEK'S EDITION...
AND I'VE BEEN INVITED TO A SPECIAL HIGH SCHOOL NEWSPAPER PRESS CONFERENCE BEFORE HIS SHOW...
WITH AN EXTRA TICKET FOR A FRIEND!

THE STEPFORD SENTINEL

Bringing You All the News from Stepford Preparatory Academy

Sun D'Arc in Chicagoland for World Tour!

by Class President Sylvia Martin

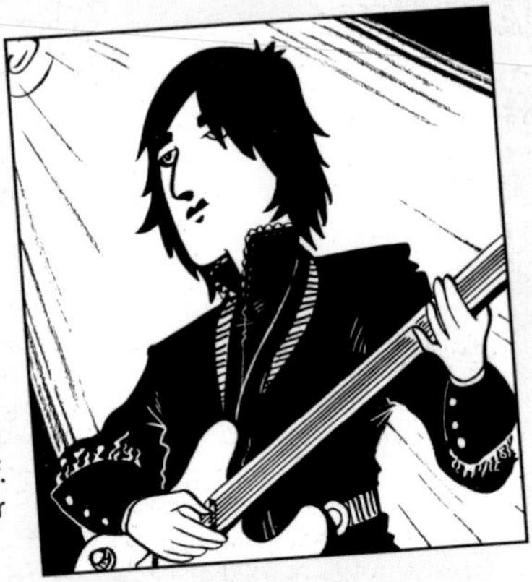

The halls of Stepford Prep are seething with excitement because superstar singer Sun D'Arc is coming to our own Chicagoland! Mr. D'Arc's manager, Vora Schak, has sent two tickets to the journalism department of every Chicagoland high school, inviting teen reporters to a special school newspaper conference before his show. Mr. D'Arc has a special bond with all teenagers because, at 18, he is still a teen himself. Stepford Prep will be represented at the conference by our beloved poetry editor, Megan Yamamura, and a friend.

No Running on Stairs

by Class President Sylvia Martin

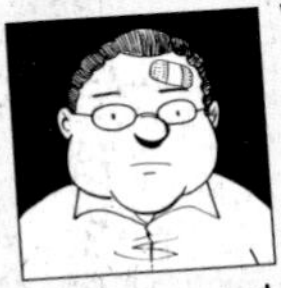

Yesterday, one of our students, Otto Van Blick, was injured when two students running on the stairs knocked into him. Otto suffered a sprained wrist and was sent home, where we all hope he recovers quickly. The two students, who shall remain nameless, were also sent home, where we hope they will meditate on the damage they have done. We hope that all the students will learn from this sad lesson: running on the stairs is dangerous and can lead to sprained wrists and other disorders.

Otto's mother, Mrs. Van Blick, hopes that one of Otto's friends will bring him his homework.

Two Haiku on Sun D'Arc

by Megan Yamamura, poetry editor

I

O Sun, shine D'Arcly!
Your guitar sadly whimpers
Singing its sorrow.

II

O Sun, my dark moon!
Only I, a teenaged girl,
Share your suffering.

INQUIRING REPORTER

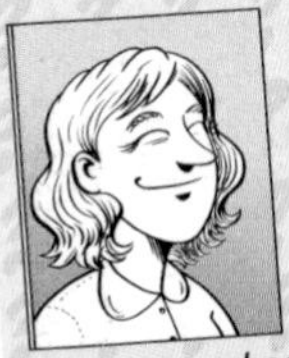

by Class President Sylvia Martin

This week's Inquiring Reporter question is:

When our school has special tickets to give out for major events, like, for instance, a press conference with a cool rock star, do you think it's fair that the teachers can decide who to give the tickets to, just because, say, somebody wrote a poem or something, or should there be a lottery, so everybody has a chance?

Your opinions will be printed in the next issue.

Introducing Jazmin Farid!

by Class President Sylvia Martin

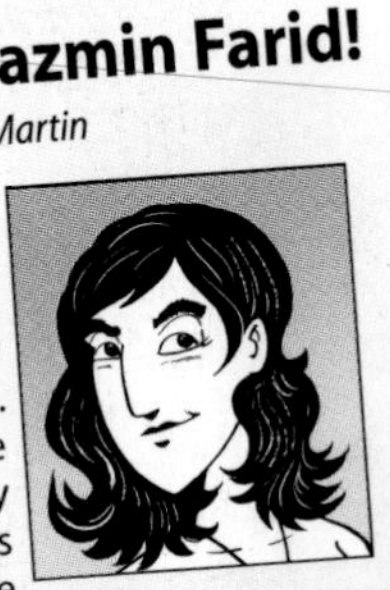

We hope everybody at Stepford Prep will give a rousing welcome to our new student Jazmin Farid. Jazmin hails all the way from sunny Egypt. Jazmin's faves are rocky road ice cream, long walks on the beach, and the superstar singer Sun D'Arc. Let's all show Jazmin that famous Stepford hospitality!

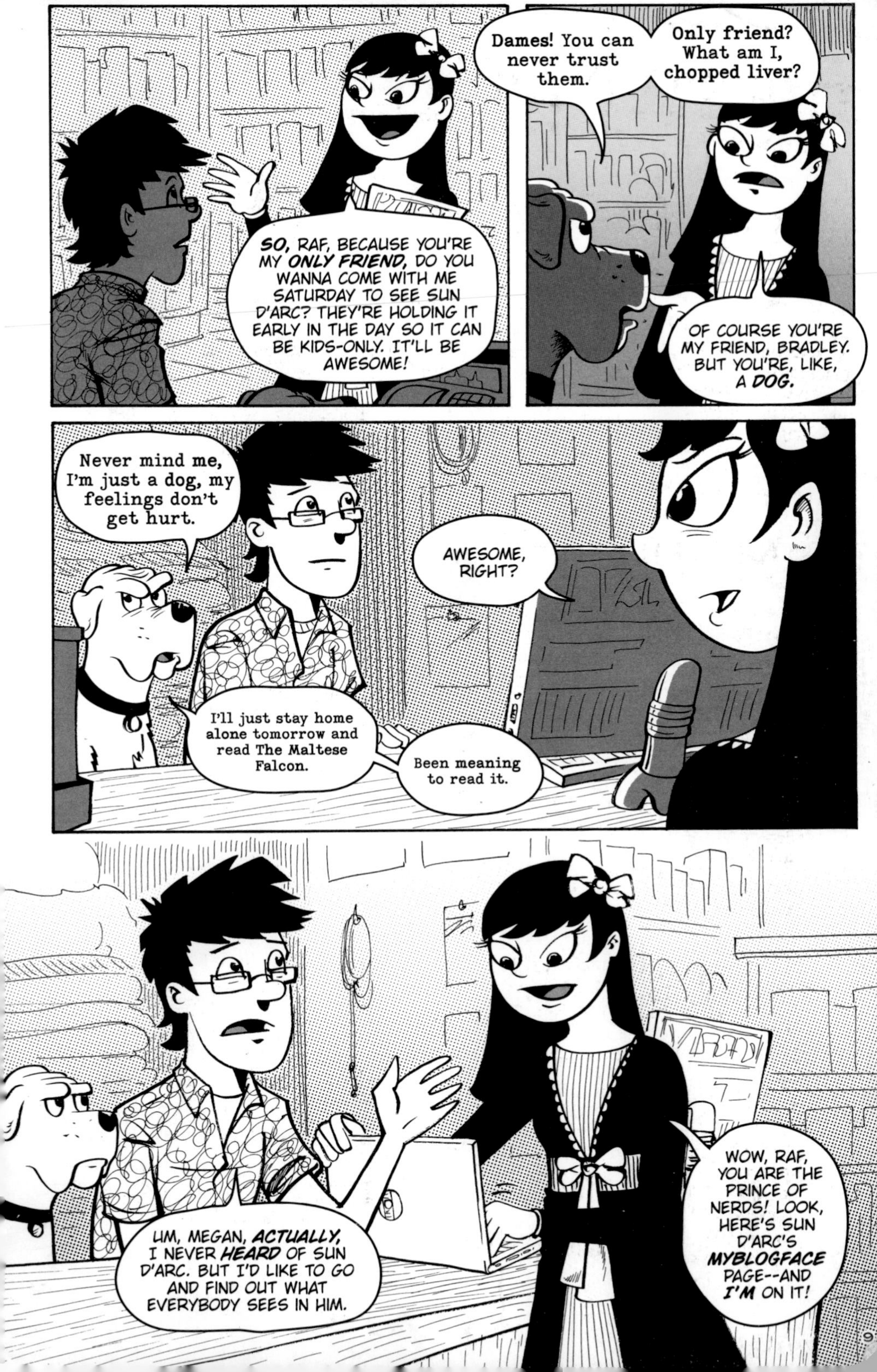
SO, RAF, BECAUSE YOU'RE MY ONLY FRIEND, DO YOU WANNA COME WITH ME SATURDAY TO SEE SUN D'ARC? THEY'RE HOLDING IT EARLY IN THE DAY SO IT CAN BE KIDS-ONLY. IT'LL BE AWESOME!
Dames! You can never trust them.
Only friend? What am I, chopped liver?
OF COURSE YOU'RE MY FRIEND, BRADLEY. BUT YOU'RE, LIKE, A DOG.
Never mind me, I'm just a dog, my feelings don't get hurt.
AWESOME, RIGHT?
I'll just stay home alone tomorrow and read The Maltese Falcon.
Been meaning to read it.
UM, MEGAN, ACTUALLY, I NEVER HEARD OF SUN D'ARC. BUT I'D LIKE TO GO AND FIND OUT WHAT EVERYBODY SEES IN HIM.
WOW, RAF, YOU ARE THE PRINCE OF NERDS! LOOK, HERE'S SUN D'ARC'S MYBLOGFACE PAGE--AND I'M ON IT!

MYBLOGFACE

Meet the FACE

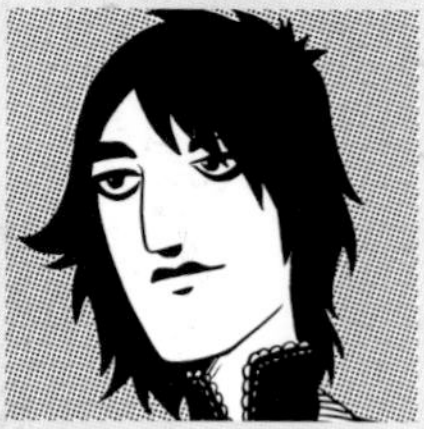

Sun D'Arc
Age: 18 years old but with a 2,000-year-old soul.

"The world is my home, and all its sorrow."

Latest hit: "U Fly With Me, Broken Bird."

Friendly FACErs

90,233,960 Friends

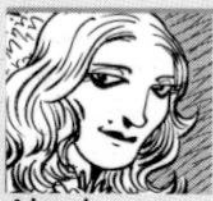
Altadonna

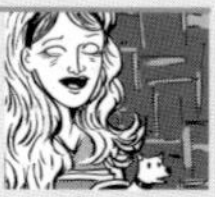
London

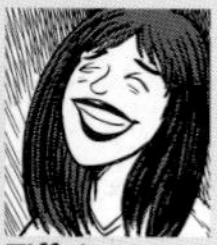
Tiffni

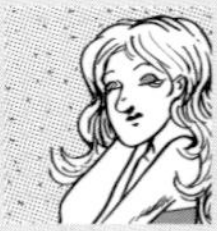
Annie Missouri

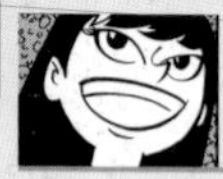

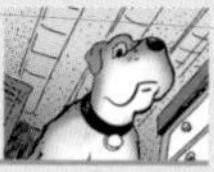

Sun D'Arc's Bio

Interests:
Meditating on the sorrows of a foolish world, black lace on my shirts made to order by nuns at a convent in the south of France, watching the crows flock at eventide along the Thames, reading the obituaries, black boots custom made in Italy, long walks on the beach, and rocky road ice cream.

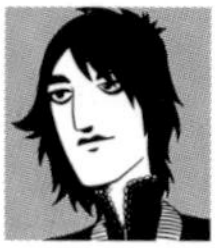

Sun D'Arc Check out my new vid for "U Fly With Me, Broken Bird." Peace.

September 6 at 1:15 PM

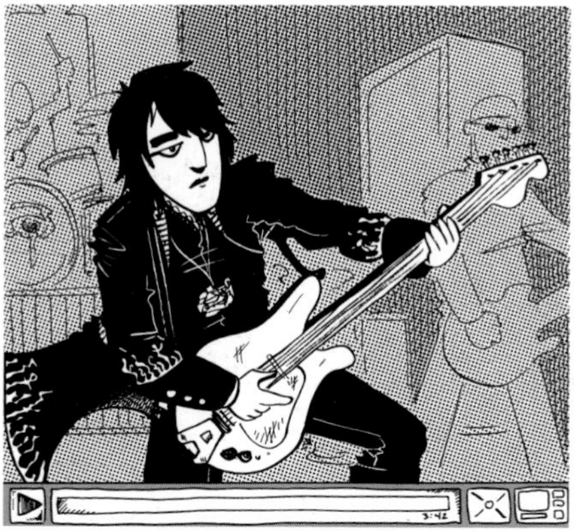

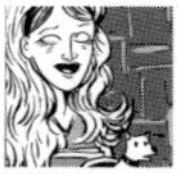

London: I love you, Sun D'Arc, but please give back my daddy's hotel. I didn't mean to give it to you for keeps, it was only a loan, and Daddy's asking about it.

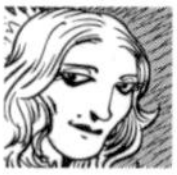

Altadonna: Do you think you could go for an older woman?

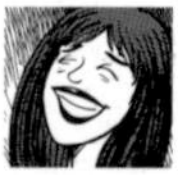

Tiffni: You promised we had a date. Why did you stand me up? My heart is breaking!

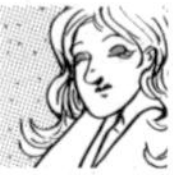

Annie Missouri: I never knew the delicious torture of love till I met you!

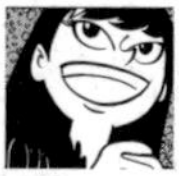

Megan Yamamura: Hi, it's me, Megan! I'm your biggest fan and I've sent you six hundred haiku!

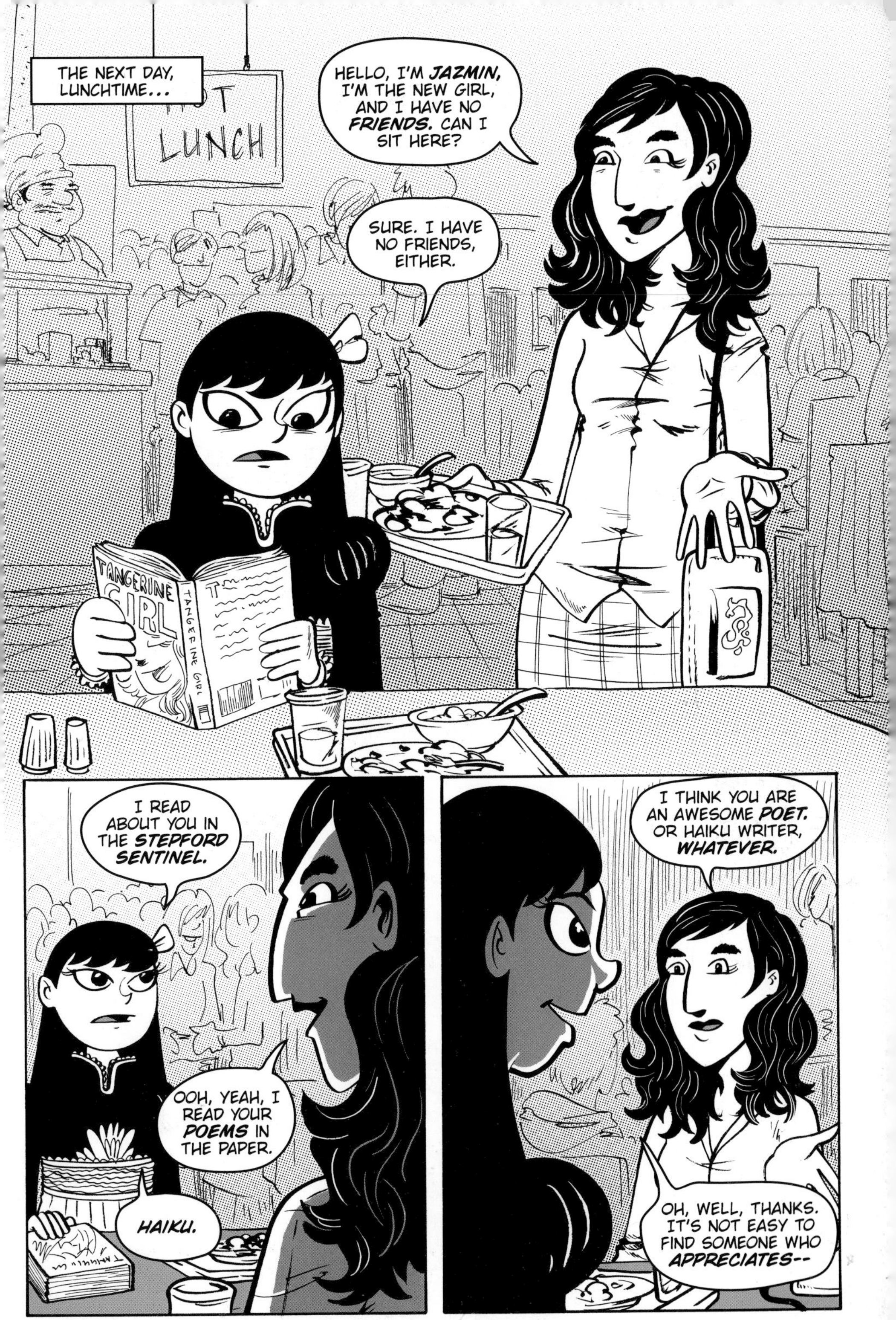
THE NEXT DAY, LUNCHTIME...
LUNCH
HELLO, I'M JAZMIN, I'M THE NEW GIRL, AND I HAVE NO FRIENDS. CAN I SIT HERE?
SURE. I HAVE NO FRIENDS, EITHER.
TANGERINE GIRL
TANGERINE GIRL
I READ ABOUT YOU IN THE STEPFORD SENTINEL.
OOH, YEAH, I READ YOUR POEMS IN THE PAPER.
HAIKU.
I THINK YOU ARE AN AWESOME POET. OR HAIKU WRITER, WHATEVER.
OH, WELL, THANKS. IT'S NOT EASY TO FIND SOMEONE WHO APPRECIATES--

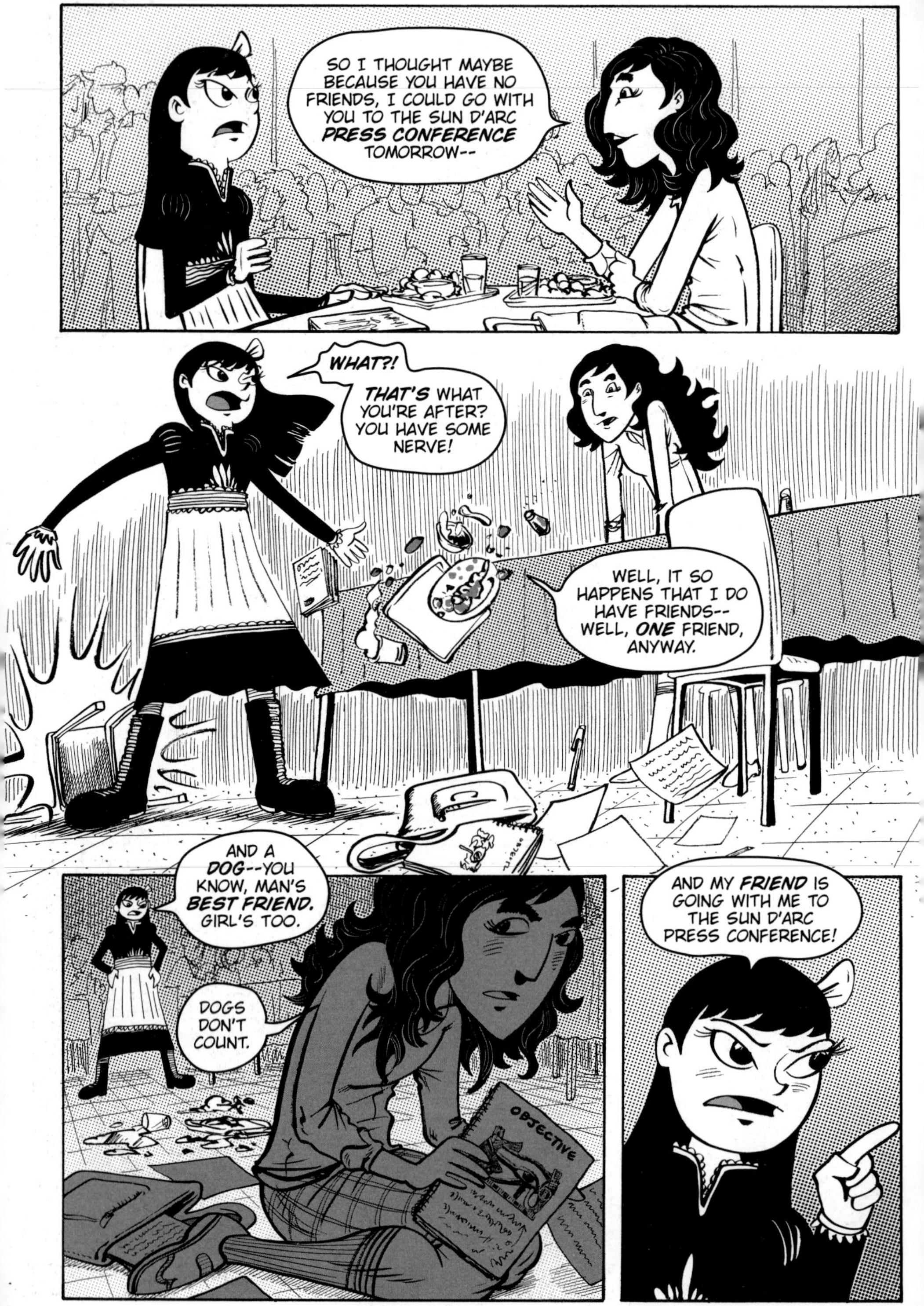
SO I THOUGHT MAYBE BECAUSE YOU HAVE NO FRIENDS, I COULD GO WITH YOU TO THE SUN D'ARC PRESS CONFERENCE TOMORROW--
WHAT?! THAT'S WHAT YOU'RE AFTER? YOU HAVE SOME NERVE!
WELL, IT SO HAPPENS THAT I DO HAVE FRIENDS-- WELL, ONE FRIEND, ANYWAY.
AND A DOG--YOU KNOW, MAN'S BEST FRIEND. GIRL'S TOO.
DOGS DON'T COUNT.
OBJECTIVE
AND MY FRIEND IS GOING WITH ME TO THE SUN D'ARC PRESS CONFERENCE!

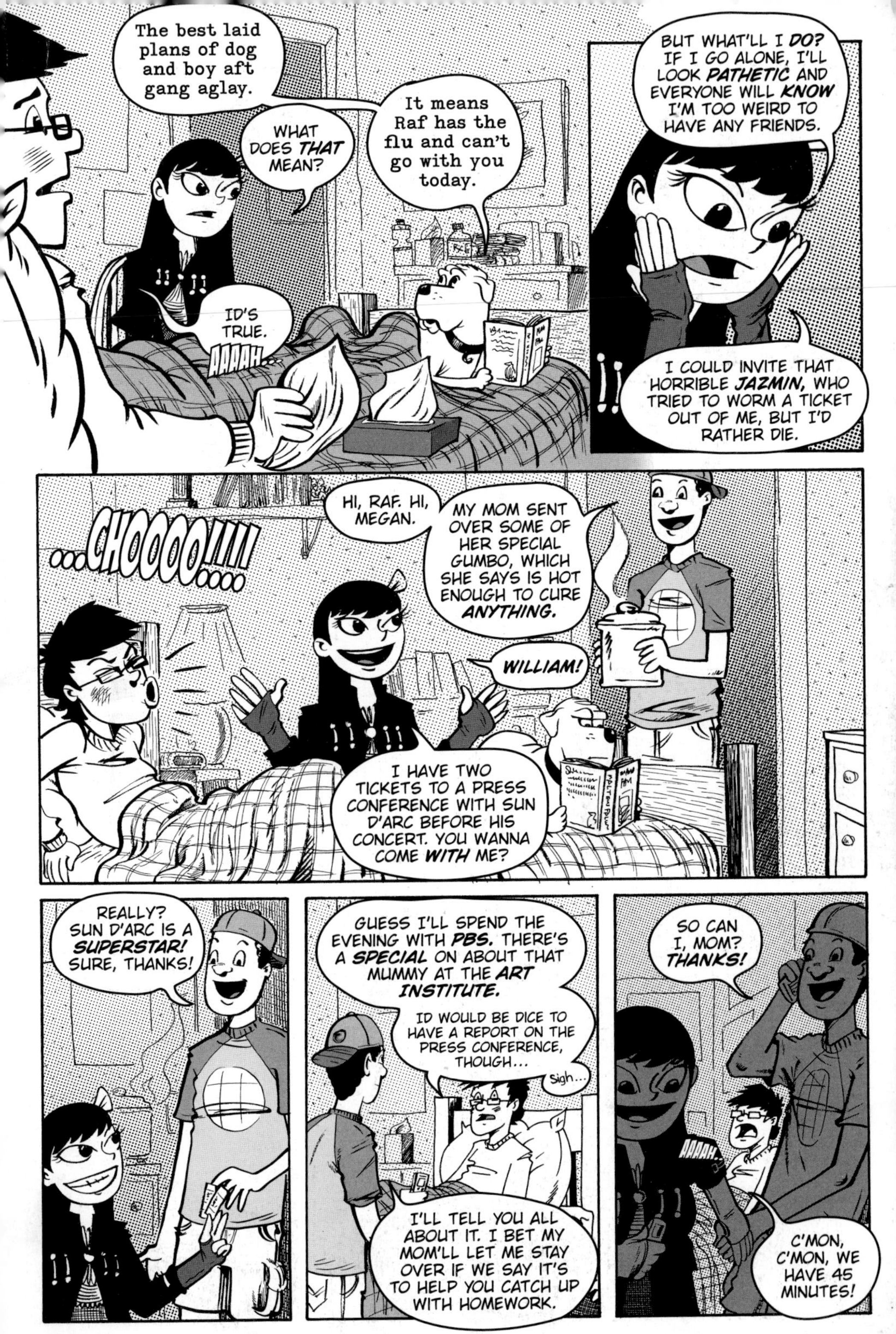

The best laid plans of dog and boy aft gang aglay.
WHAT DOES THAT MEAN?
It means Raf has the flu and can't go with you today.
ID'S TRUE.
AAAAH
BUT WHAT'LL I DO? IF I GO ALONE, I'LL LOOK PATHETIC AND EVERYONE WILL KNOW I'M TOO WEIRD TO HAVE ANY FRIENDS.
I COULD INVITE THAT HORRIBLE JAZMIN, WHO TRIED TO WORM A TICKET OUT OF ME, BUT I'D RATHER DIE.
...CHOOOO!!!!...oooo
HI, RAF. HI, MEGAN.
MY MOM SENT OVER SOME OF HER SPECIAL GUMBO, WHICH SHE SAYS IS HOT ENOUGH TO CURE ANYTHING.
WILLIAM!
I HAVE TWO TICKETS TO A PRESS CONFERENCE WITH SUN D'ARC BEFORE HIS CONCERT. YOU WANNA COME WITH ME?
REALLY? SUN D'ARC IS A SUPERSTAR! SURE, THANKS!
GUESS I'LL SPEND THE EVENING WITH PBS. THERE'S A SPECIAL ON ABOUT THAT MUMMY AT THE ART INSTITUTE.
ID WOULD BE DICE TO HAVE A REPORT ON THE PRESS CONFERENCE, THOUGH...
Sigh...
I'LL TELL YOU ALL ABOUT IT. I BET MY MOM'LL LET ME STAY OVER IF WE SAY IT'S TO HELP YOU CATCH UP WITH HOMEWORK.
SO CAN I, MOM? THANKS!
AAAAH
C'MON, C'MON, WE HAVE 45 MINUTES!

CHAPTER TWO: SHADOW OF A DOUBT

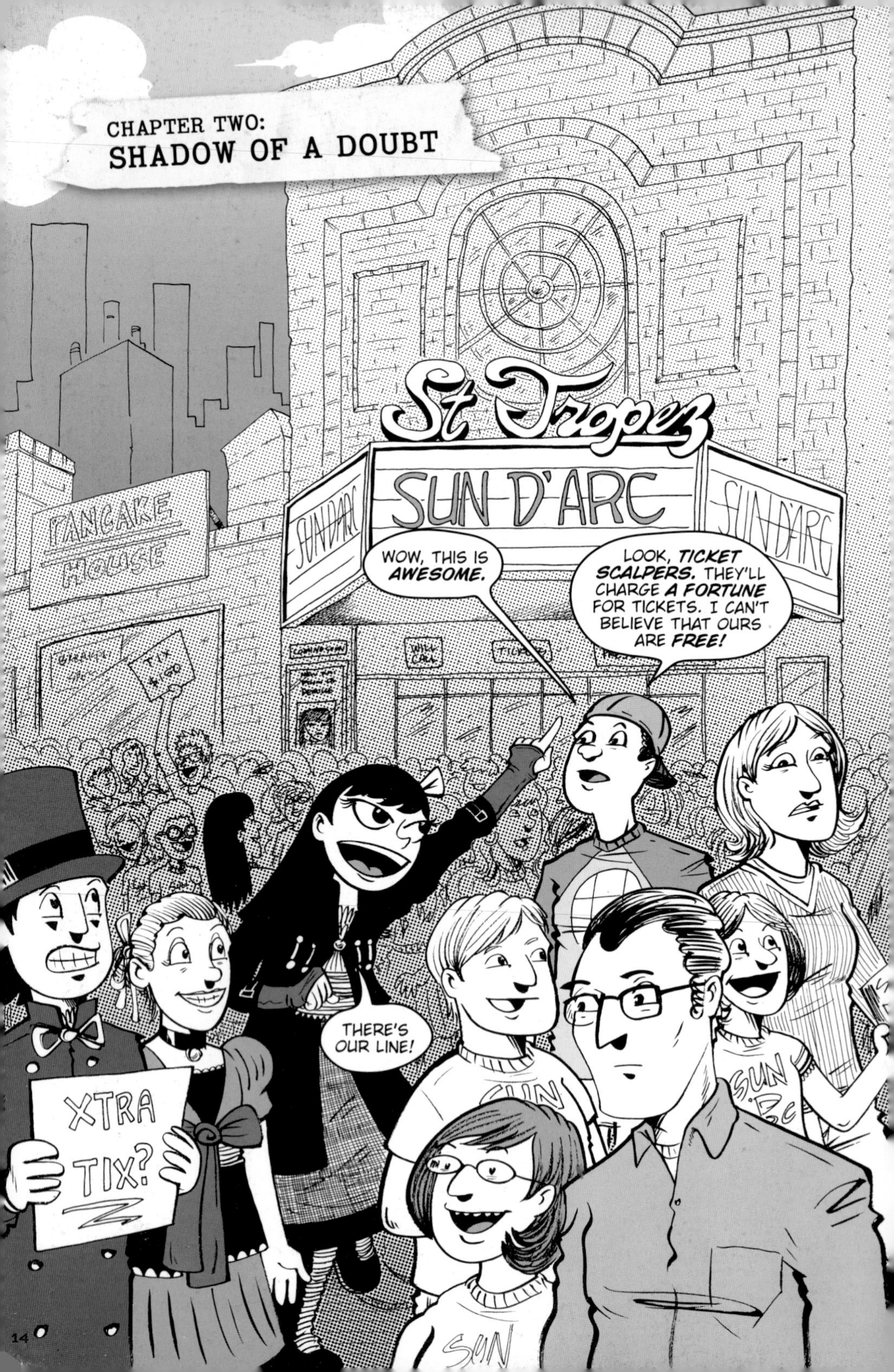
St Tropez
SUN D'ARC
PANCAKE HOUSE
WOW, THIS IS **AWESOME.**
LOOK, ***TICKET SCALPERS.*** THEY'LL CHARGE ***A FORTUNE*** FOR TICKETS. I CAN'T BELIEVE THAT OURS ARE ***FREE!***
THERE'S OUR LINE!
XTRA TIX?

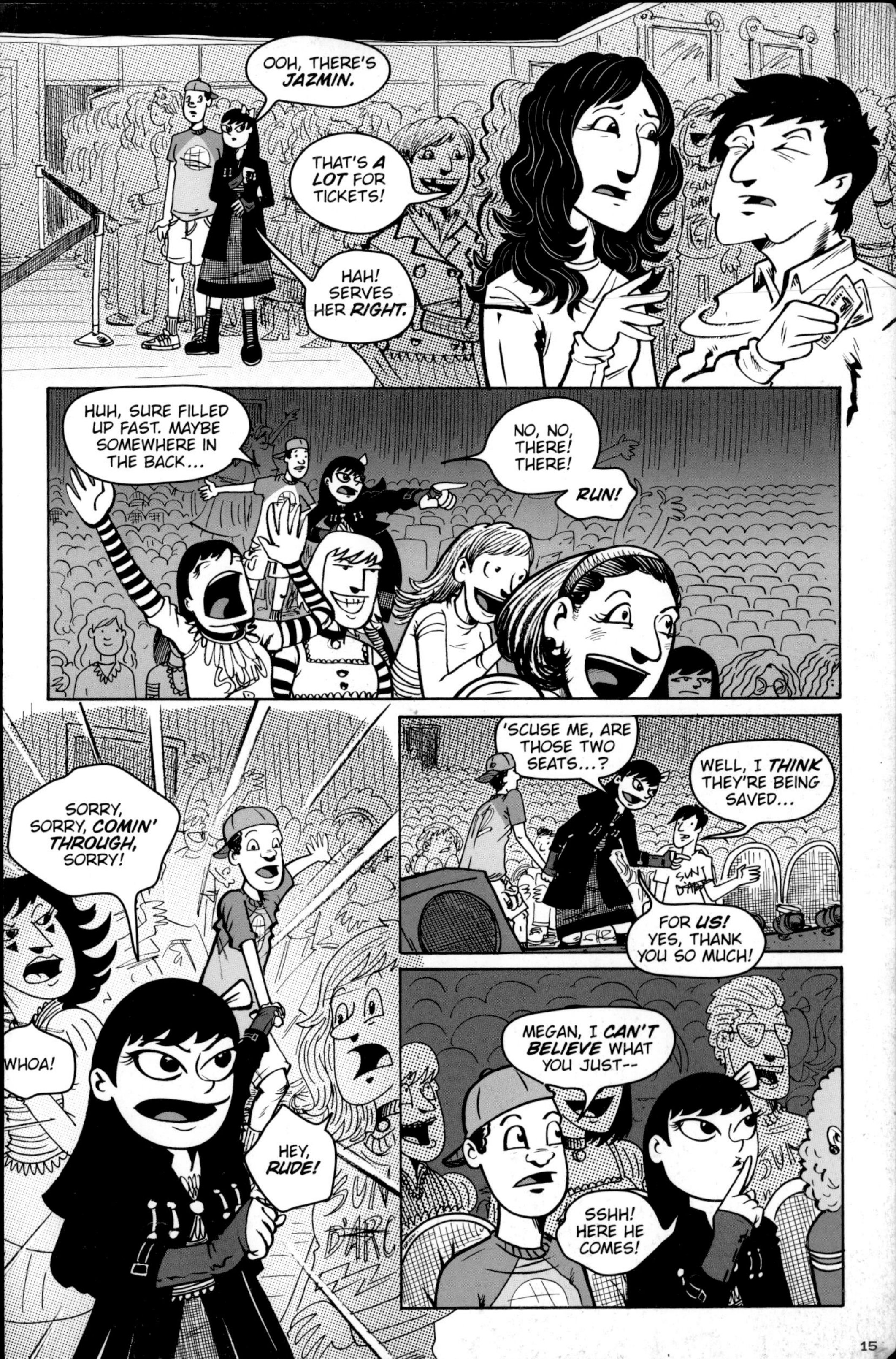
OOH, THERE'S JAZMIN.
THAT'S A LOT FOR TICKETS!
HAH! SERVES HER RIGHT.
HUH, SURE FILLED UP FAST. MAYBE SOMEWHERE IN THE BACK...
NO, NO, THERE! THERE!
RUN!
SORRY, SORRY, COMIN' THROUGH, SORRY!
WHOA!
HEY, RUDE!
'SCUSE ME, ARE THOSE TWO SEATS...?
WELL, I THINK THEY'RE BEING SAVED...
FOR US! YES, THANK YOU SO MUCH!
MEGAN, I CAN'T BELIEVE WHAT YOU JUST--
SSHH! HERE HE COMES!

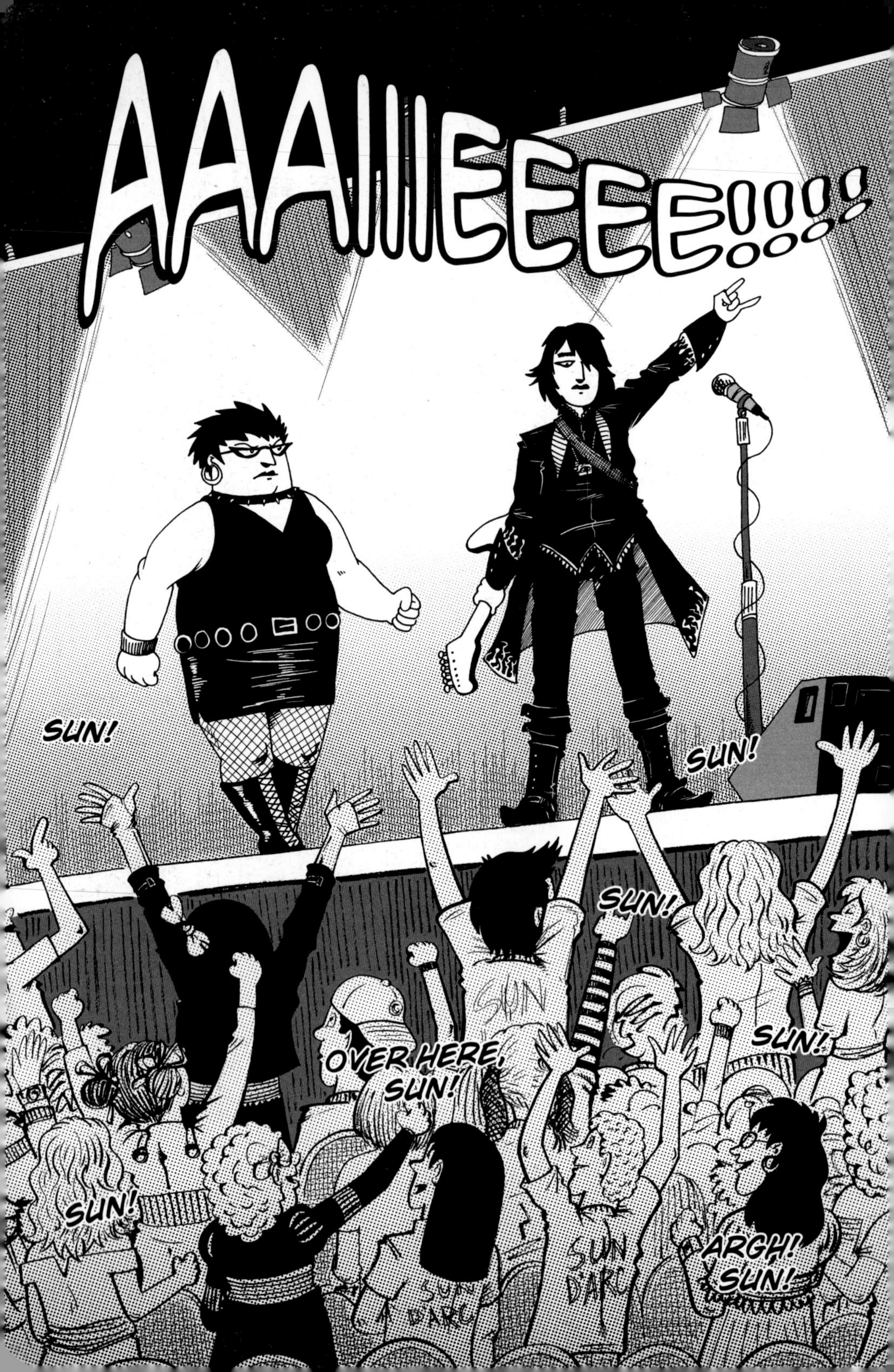
AAAIIIEEEEE!!!!!
SUN!
SUN!
SUN!
OVER HERE, SUN!
SUN!
SUN!
ARGH! SUN!

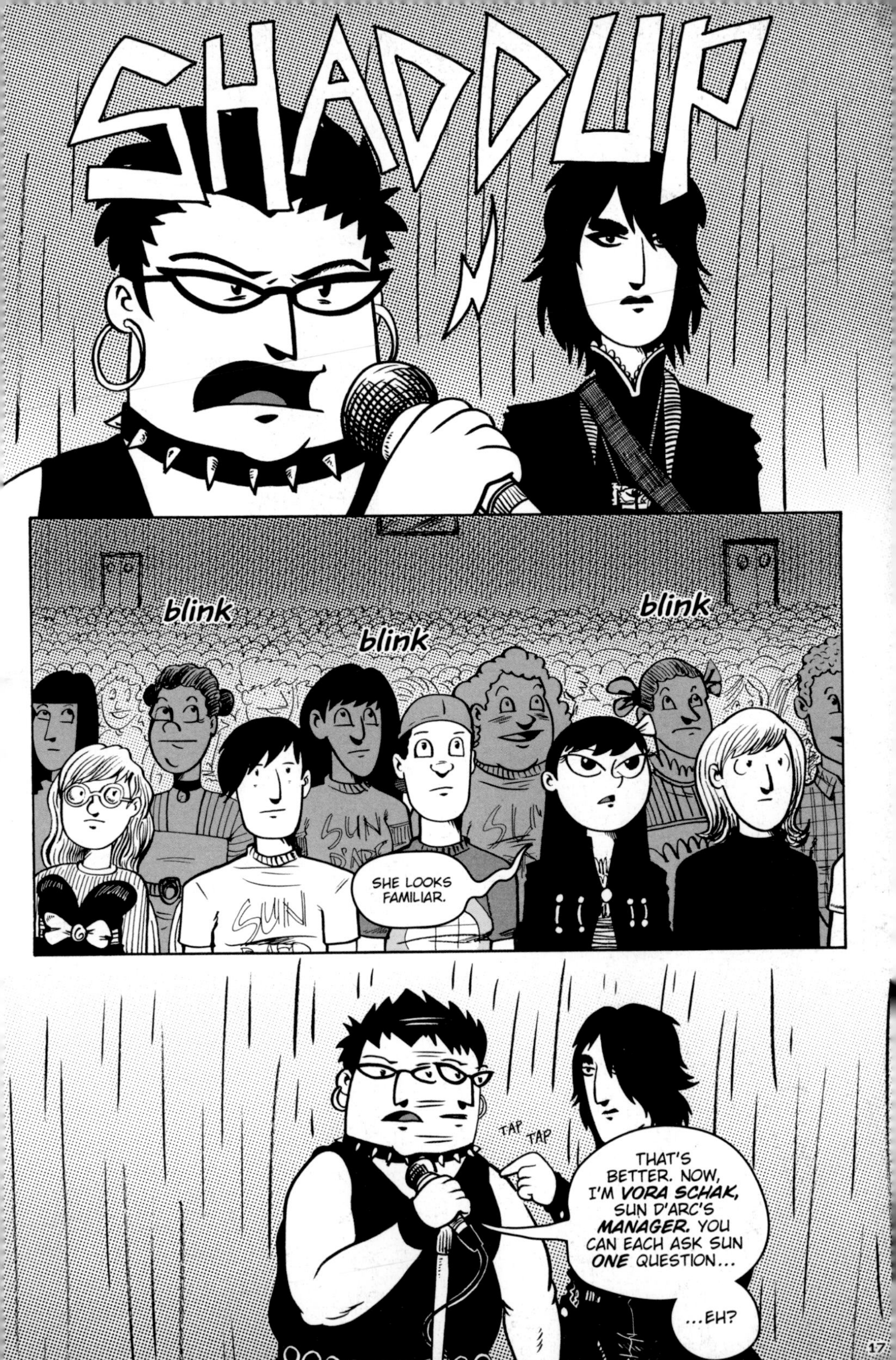
SHADDUP
blink
blink
blink
SHE LOOKS FAMILIAR.
TAP TAP
THAT'S BETTER. NOW, I'M VORA SCHAK, SUN D'ARC'S MANAGER. YOU CAN EACH ASK SUN ONE QUESTION...
...EH?

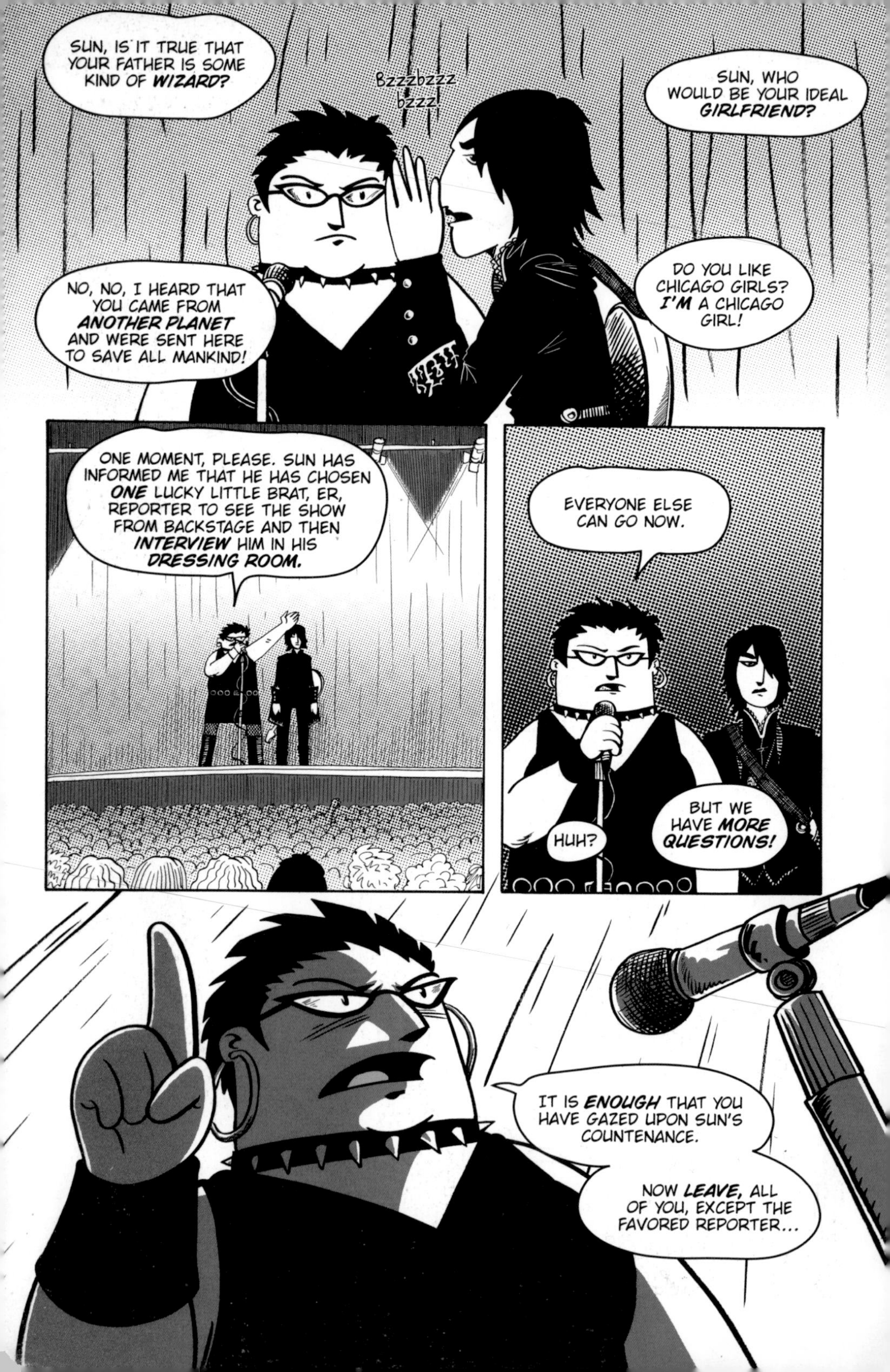
SUN, IS IT TRUE THAT YOUR FATHER IS SOME KIND OF WIZARD?
Bzzzbzzz bzzz!
SUN, WHO WOULD BE YOUR IDEAL GIRLFRIEND?
NO, NO, I HEARD THAT YOU CAME FROM ANOTHER PLANET AND WERE SENT HERE TO SAVE ALL MANKIND!
DO YOU LIKE CHICAGO GIRLS? I'M A CHICAGO GIRL!
ONE MOMENT, PLEASE. SUN HAS INFORMED ME THAT HE HAS CHOSEN ONE LUCKY LITTLE BRAT, ER, REPORTER TO SEE THE SHOW FROM BACKSTAGE AND THEN INTERVIEW HIM IN HIS DRESSING ROOM.
EVERYONE ELSE CAN GO NOW.
HUH?
BUT WE HAVE MORE QUESTIONS!
IT IS ENOUGH THAT YOU HAVE GAZED UPON SUN'S COUNTENANCE.
NOW LEAVE, ALL OF YOU, EXCEPT THE FAVORED REPORTER...

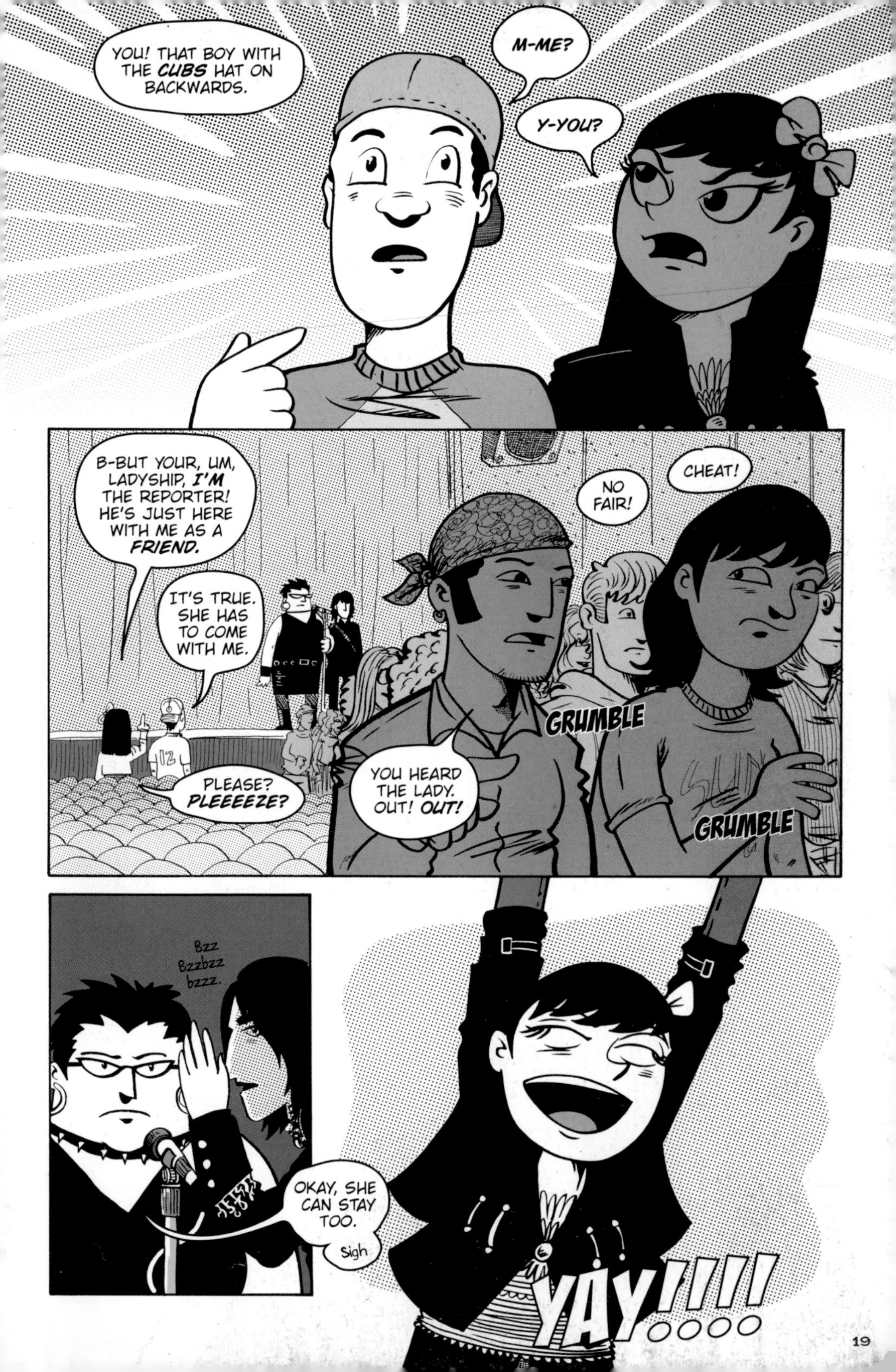

YOU! THAT BOY WITH THE CUBS HAT ON BACKWARDS.
M-ME?
Y-YOU?
B-BUT YOUR, UM, LADYSHIP, I'M THE REPORTER! HE'S JUST HERE WITH ME AS A FRIEND.
IT'S TRUE. SHE HAS TO COME WITH ME.
PLEASE? PLEEEEZE?
NO FAIR!
CHEAT!
YOU HEARD THE LADY. OUT! OUT!
GRUMBLE
GRUMBLE
Bzz Bzzbzz bzzz.
OKAY, SHE CAN STAY TOO.
Sigh
YAY!!!!!OOOO

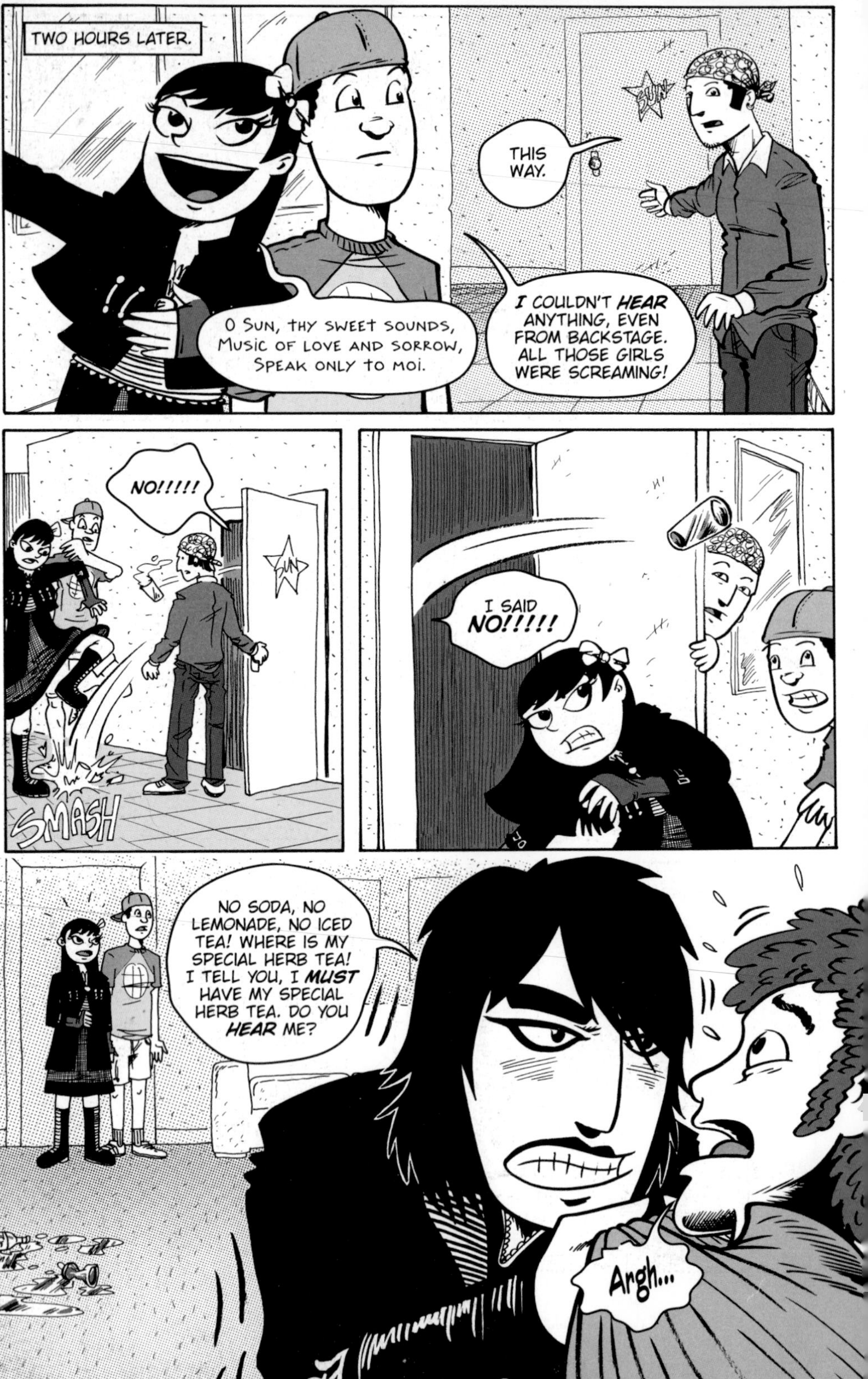
TWO HOURS LATER.
O Sun, thy sweet sounds, Music of love and sorrow, Speak only to moi.
THIS WAY.
I COULDN'T HEAR ANYTHING, EVEN FROM BACKSTAGE. ALL THOSE GIRLS WERE SCREAMING!
NO!!!!!
SUN
SMASH
I SAID NO!!!!!
NO SODA, NO LEMONADE, NO ICED TEA! WHERE IS MY SPECIAL HERB TEA! I TELL YOU, I MUST HAVE MY SPECIAL HERB TEA. DO YOU HEAR ME?
Argh...

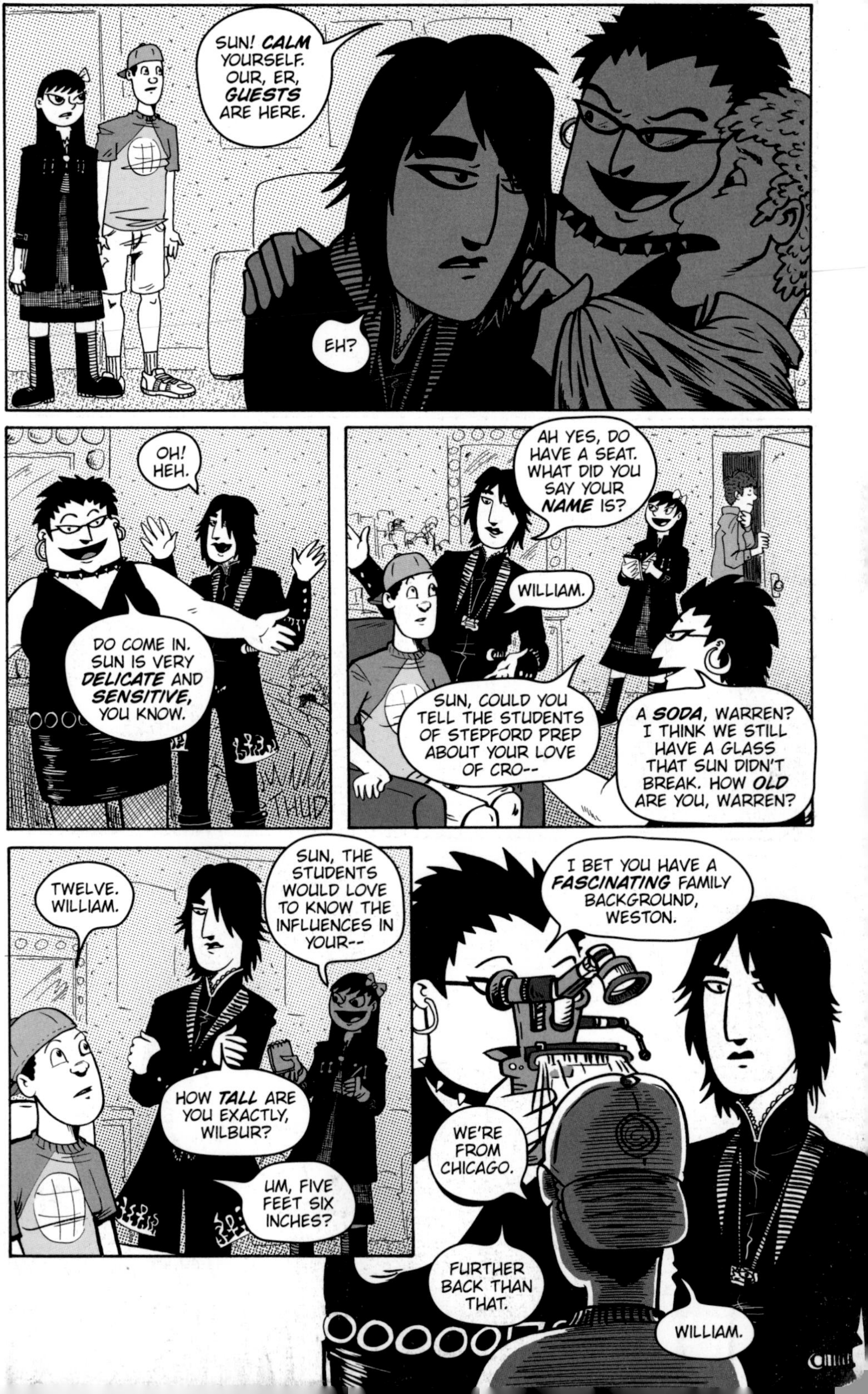
SUN! CALM YOURSELF. OUR, ER, GUESTS ARE HERE.
EH?
OH! HEH.
DO COME IN. SUN IS VERY DELICATE AND SENSITIVE, YOU KNOW.
THUD
AH YES, DO HAVE A SEAT. WHAT DID YOU SAY YOUR NAME IS?
WILLIAM.
SUN, COULD YOU TELL THE STUDENTS OF STEPFORD PREP ABOUT YOUR LOVE OF CRO--
A SODA, WARREN? I THINK WE STILL HAVE A GLASS THAT SUN DIDN'T BREAK. HOW OLD ARE YOU, WARREN?
TWELVE. WILLIAM.
SUN, THE STUDENTS WOULD LOVE TO KNOW THE INFLUENCES IN YOUR--
HOW TALL ARE YOU EXACTLY, WILBUR?
UM, FIVE FEET SIX INCHES?
I BET YOU HAVE A FASCINATING FAMILY BACKGROUND, WESTON.
WE'RE FROM CHICAGO.
FURTHER BACK THAN THAT.
WILLIAM.

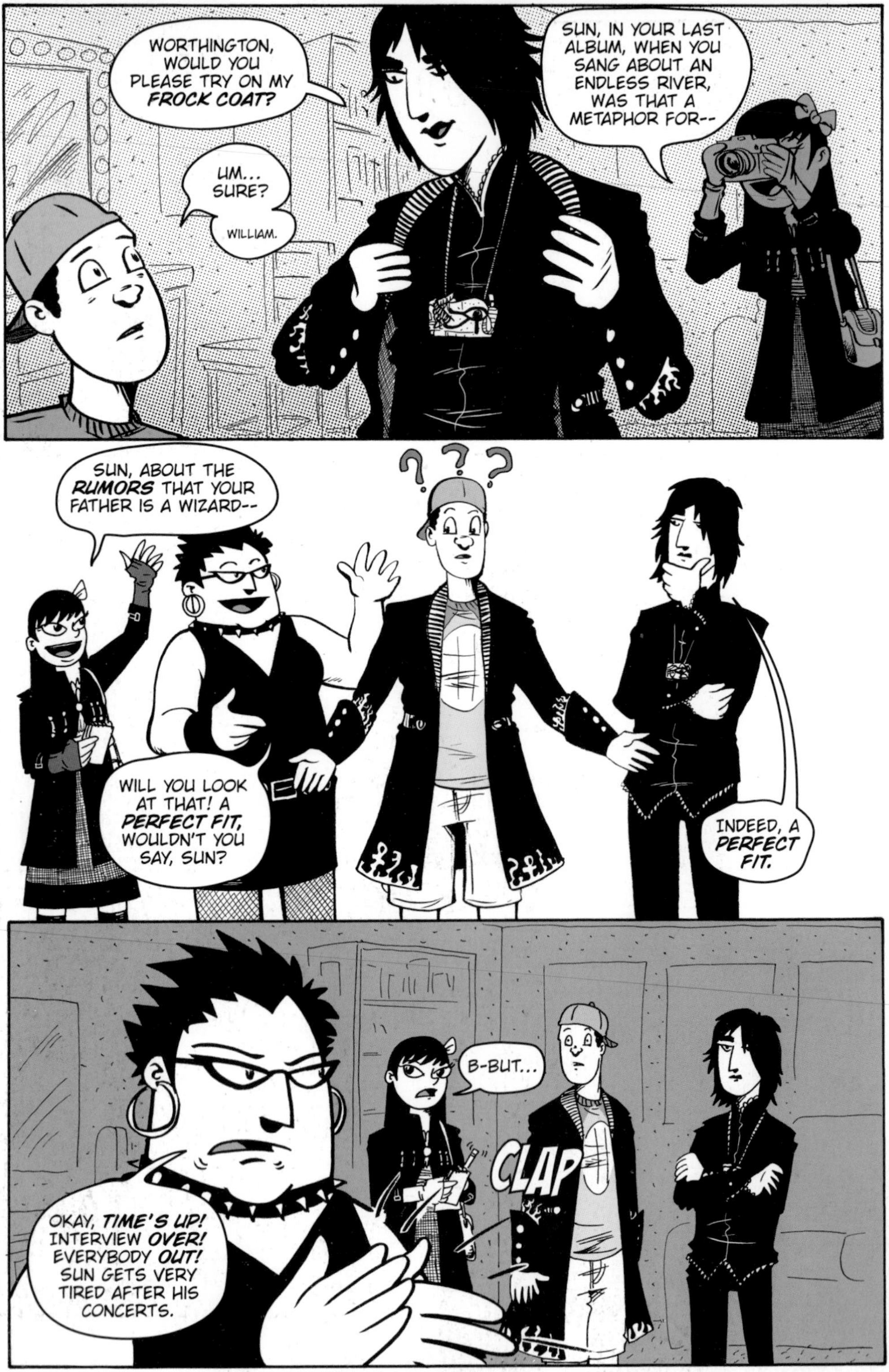
WORTHINGTON, WOULD YOU PLEASE TRY ON MY FROCK COAT?
SUN, IN YOUR LAST ALBUM, WHEN YOU SANG ABOUT AN ENDLESS RIVER, WAS THAT A METAPHOR FOR--
UM... SURE?
WILLIAM.
SUN, ABOUT THE RUMORS THAT YOUR FATHER IS A WIZARD--
? ? ?
WILL YOU LOOK AT THAT! A PERFECT FIT, WOULDN'T YOU SAY, SUN?
INDEED, A PERFECT FIT.
B-BUT...
CLAP
OKAY, TIME'S UP! INTERVIEW OVER! EVERYBODY OUT! SUN GETS VERY TIRED AFTER HIS CONCERTS.

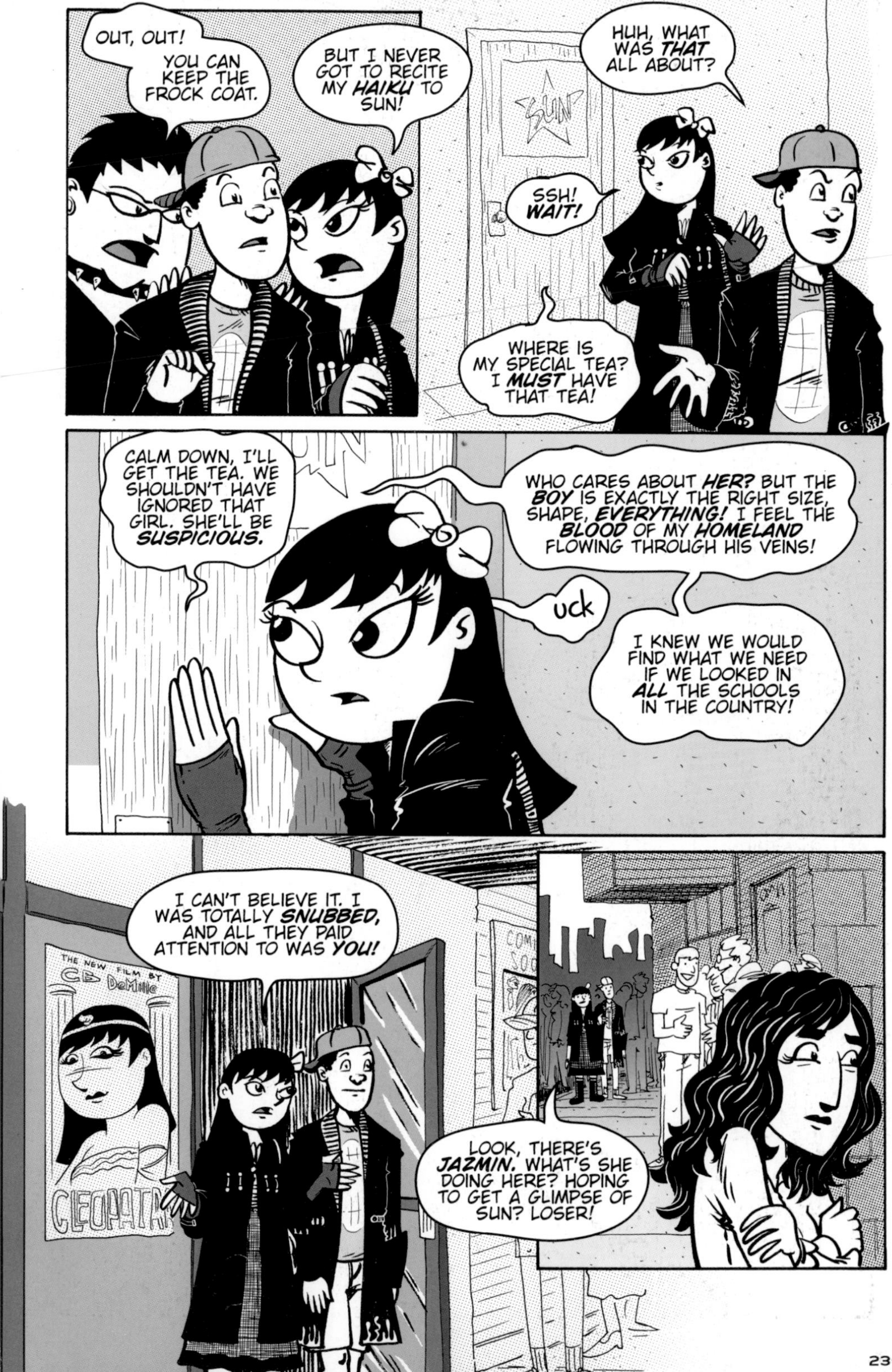
OUT, OUT!
YOU CAN KEEP THE FROCK COAT.
BUT I NEVER GOT TO RECITE MY HAIKU TO SUN!
SUN
HUH, WHAT WAS THAT ALL ABOUT?
SSH! WAIT!
WHERE IS MY SPECIAL TEA? I MUST HAVE THAT TEA!
CALM DOWN, I'LL GET THE TEA. WE SHOULDN'T HAVE IGNORED THAT GIRL. SHE'LL BE SUSPICIOUS.
WHO CARES ABOUT HER? BUT THE BOY IS EXACTLY THE RIGHT SIZE, SHAPE, EVERYTHING! I FEEL THE BLOOD OF MY HOMELAND FLOWING THROUGH HIS VEINS!
uck
I KNEW WE WOULD FIND WHAT WE NEED IF WE LOOKED IN ALL THE SCHOOLS IN THE COUNTRY!
THE NEW FILM BY CB DeMille
CLEOPATRA
I CAN'T BELIEVE IT. I WAS TOTALLY SNUBBED, AND ALL THEY PAID ATTENTION TO WAS YOU!
LOOK, THERE'S JAZMIN. WHAT'S SHE DOING HERE? HOPING TO GET A GLIMPSE OF SUN? LOSER!

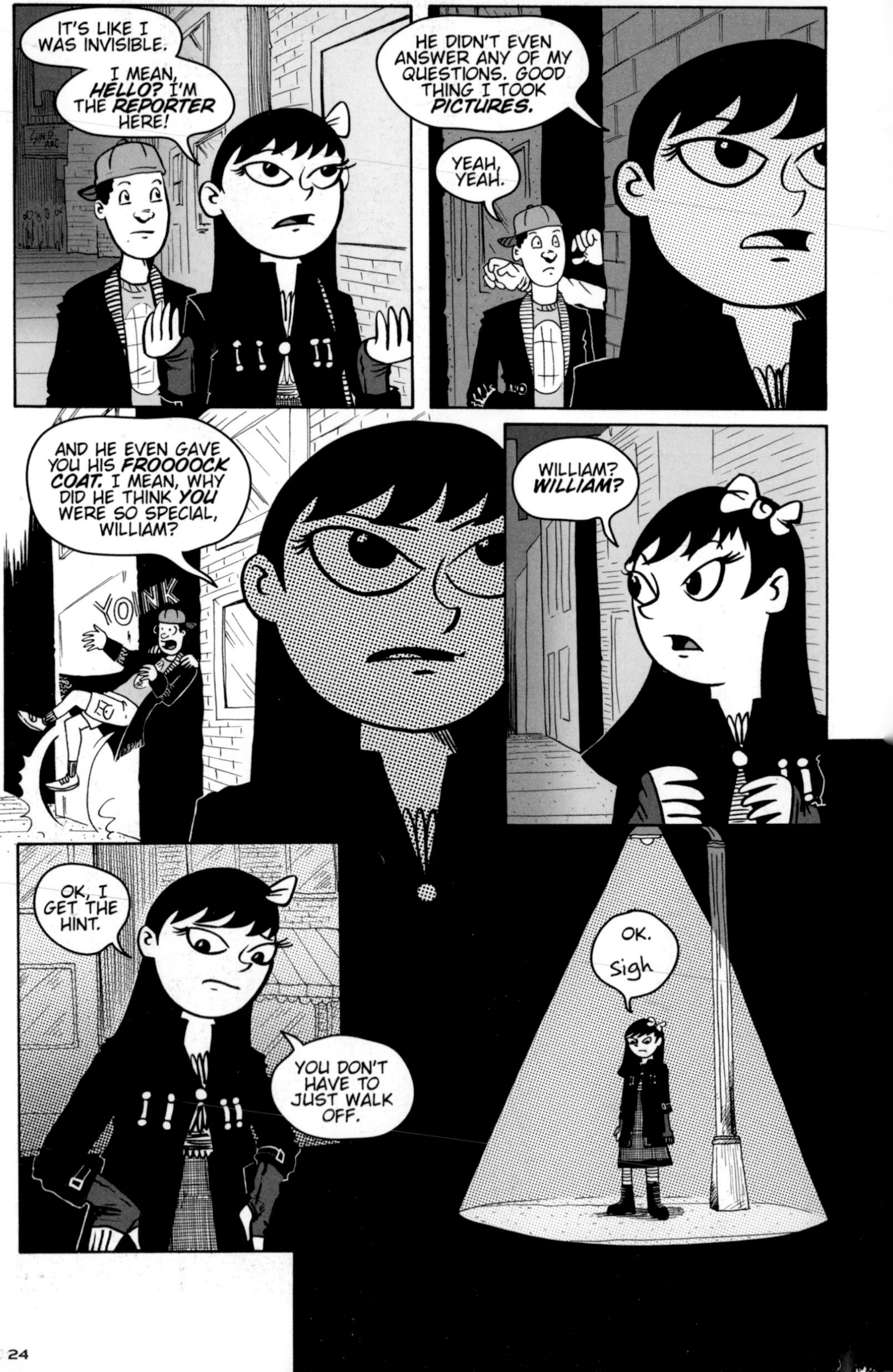
IT'S LIKE I WAS INVISIBLE.
I MEAN, *HELLO?* I'M THE *REPORTER* HERE!
HE DIDN'T EVEN ANSWER ANY OF MY QUESTIONS. GOOD THING I TOOK *PICTURES.*
YEAH, YEAH.
AND HE EVEN GAVE YOU HIS *FROOOOCK COAT.* I MEAN, WHY DID HE THINK *YOU* WERE SO SPECIAL, WILLIAM?
YOINK
WILLIAM? *WILLIAM?*
OK, I GET THE HINT.
YOU DON'T HAVE TO JUST WALK OFF.
OK.
Sigh

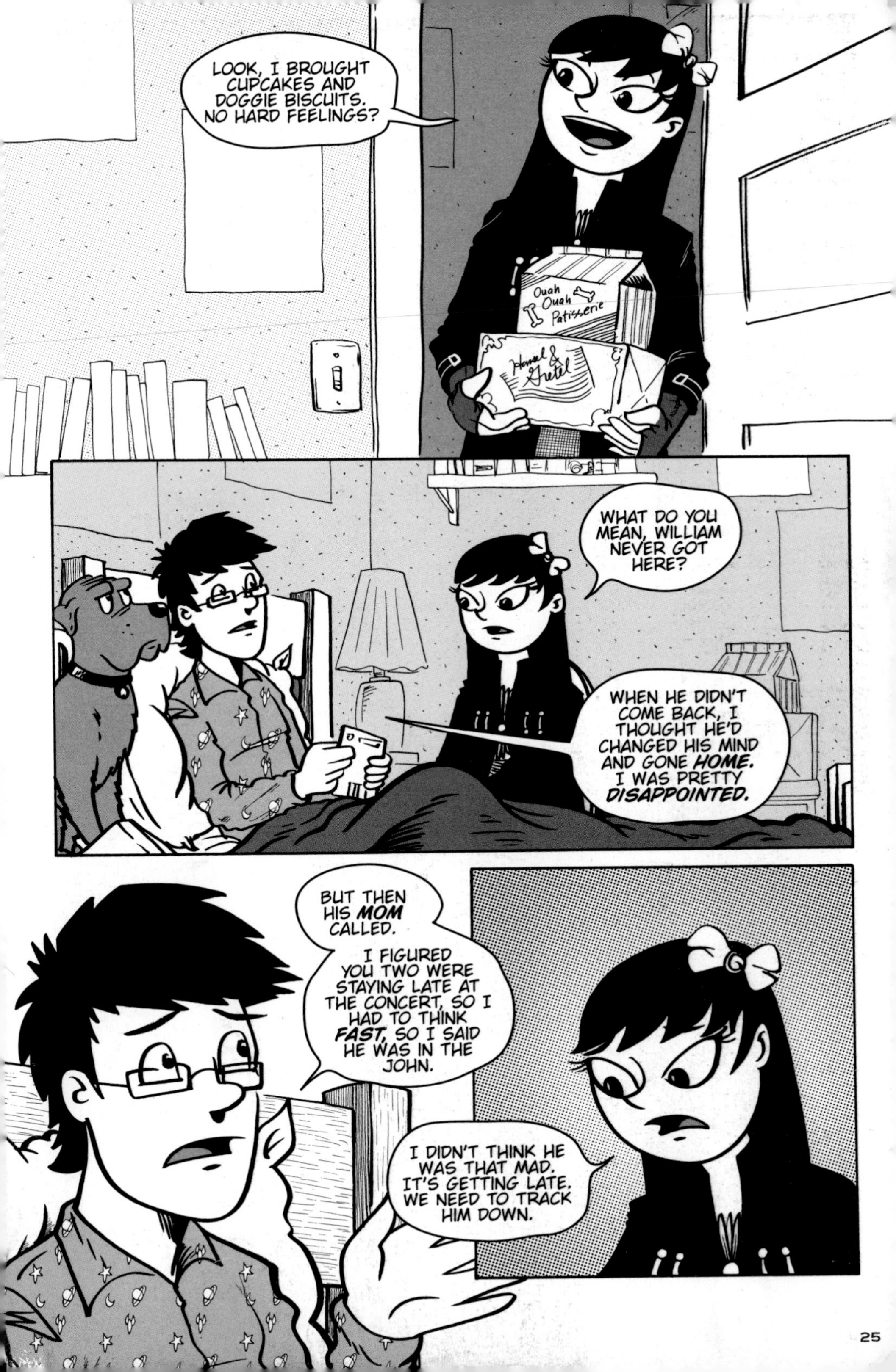
LOOK, I BROUGHT CUPCAKES AND DOGGIE BISCUITS. NO HARD FEELINGS?
Ouah Ouah Patisserie
Hansel & Gretel
WHAT DO YOU MEAN, WILLIAM NEVER GOT HERE?
WHEN HE DIDN'T COME BACK, I THOUGHT HE'D CHANGED HIS MIND AND GONE **HOME.** I WAS PRETTY **DISAPPOINTED.**
BUT THEN HIS **MOM** CALLED.
I FIGURED YOU TWO WERE STAYING LATE AT THE CONCERT, SO I HAD TO THINK **FAST,** SO I SAID HE WAS IN THE JOHN.
I DIDN'T THINK HE WAS THAT MAD. IT'S GETTING LATE. WE NEED TO TRACK HIM DOWN.

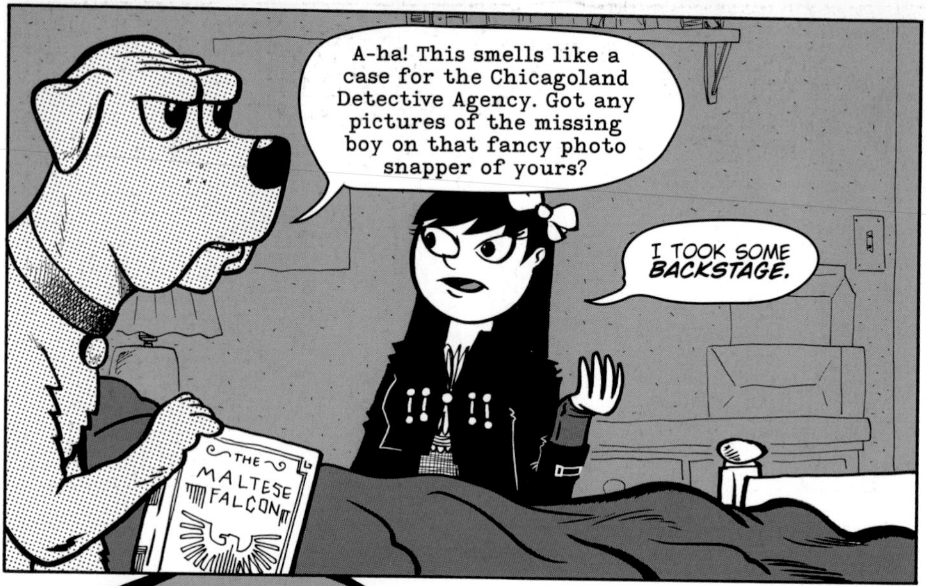
A-ha! This smells like a case for the Chicagoland Detective Agency. Got any pictures of the missing boy on that fancy photo snapper of yours?
I TOOK SOME BACKSTAGE.
THE MALTESE FALCON

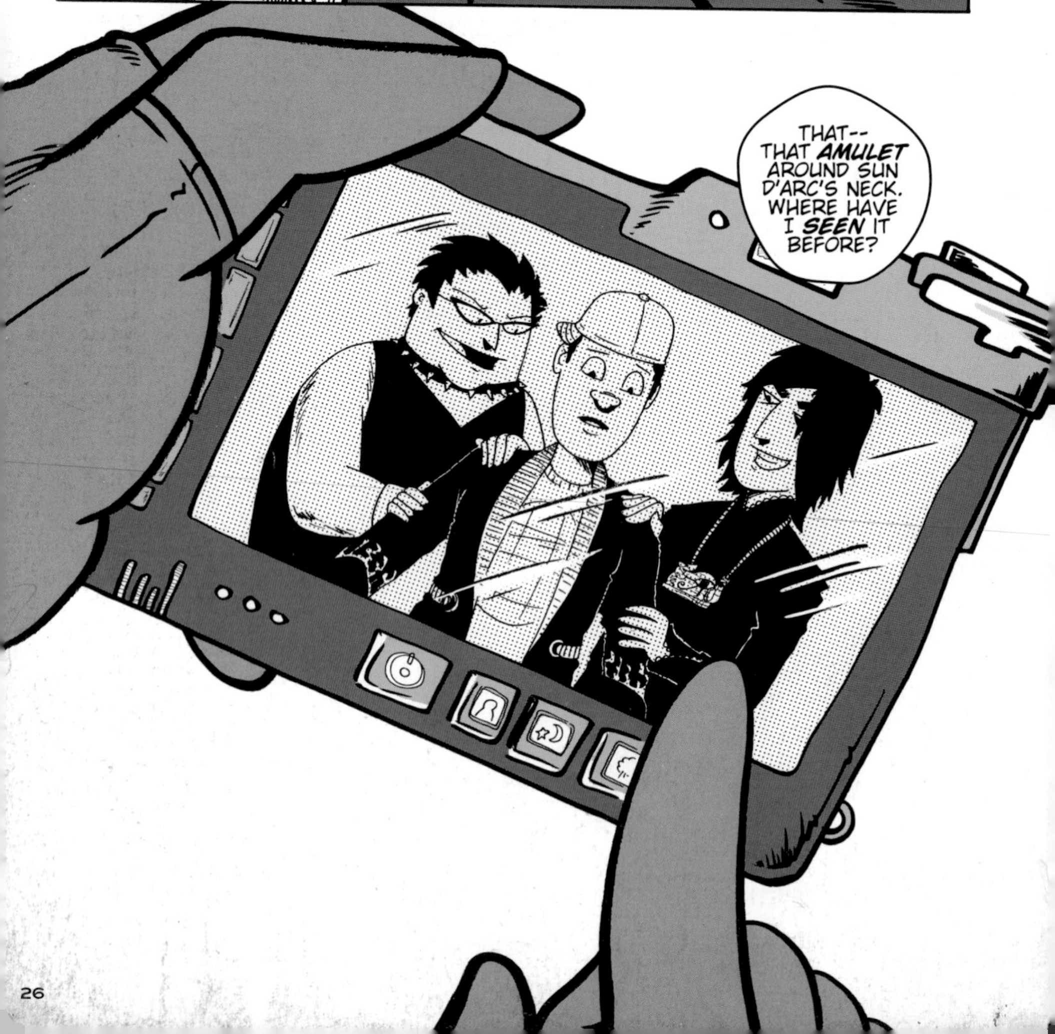
THAT-- THAT AMULET AROUND SUN D'ARC'S NECK. WHERE HAVE I SEEN IT BEFORE?

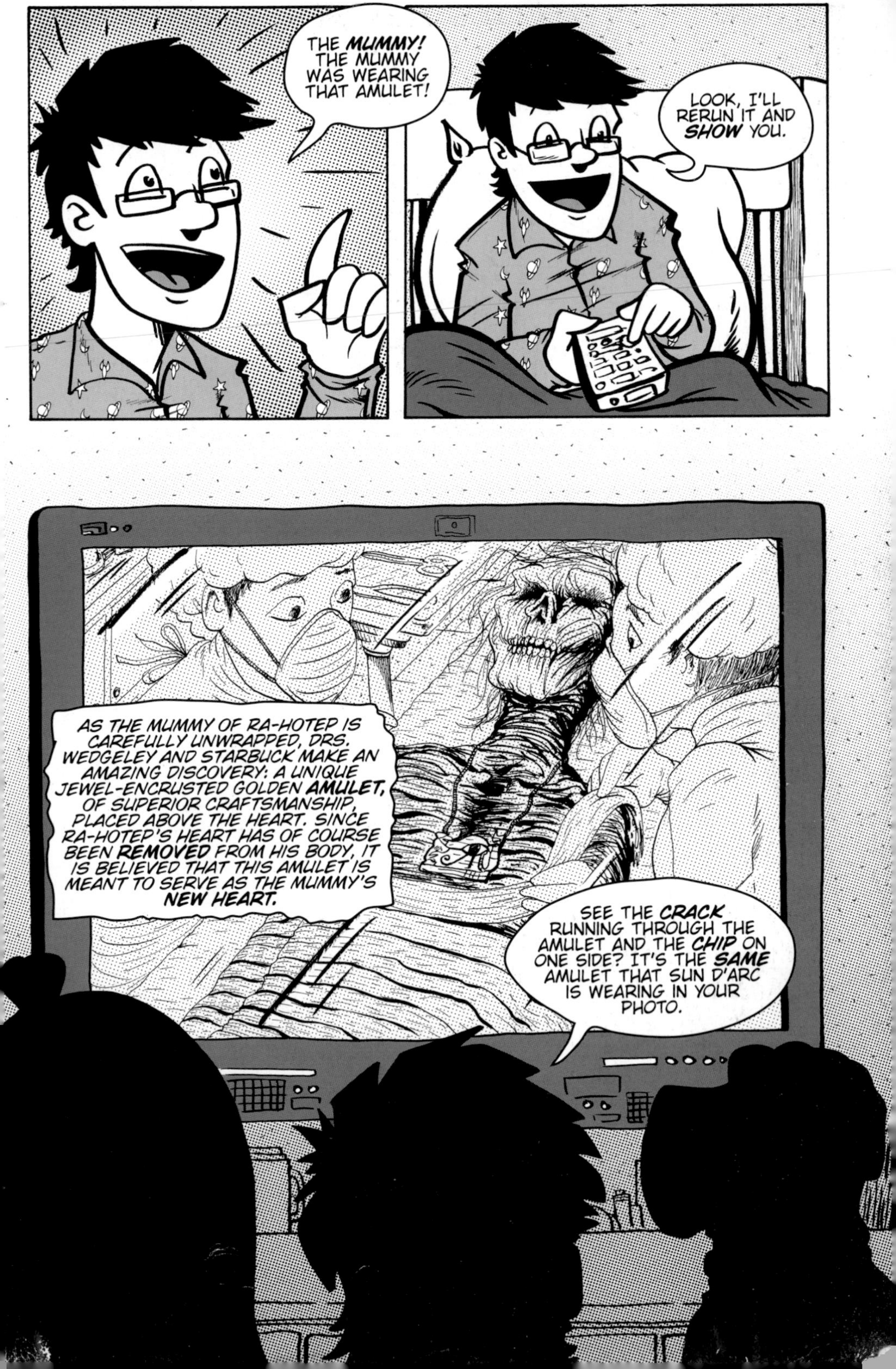
THE MUMMY! THE MUMMY WAS WEARING THAT AMULET!
LOOK, I'LL RERUN IT AND SHOW YOU.
AS THE MUMMY OF RA-HOTEP IS CAREFULLY UNWRAPPED, DRS. WEDGELEY AND STARBUCK MAKE AN AMAZING DISCOVERY: A UNIQUE JEWEL-ENCRUSTED GOLDEN AMULET, OF SUPERIOR CRAFTSMANSHIP, PLACED ABOVE THE HEART. SINCE RA-HOTEP'S HEART HAS OF COURSE BEEN REMOVED FROM HIS BODY, IT IS BELIEVED THAT THIS AMULET IS MEANT TO SERVE AS THE MUMMY'S NEW HEART.
SEE THE CRACK RUNNING THROUGH THE AMULET AND THE CHIP ON ONE SIDE? IT'S THE SAME AMULET THAT SUN D'ARC IS WEARING IN YOUR PHOTO.

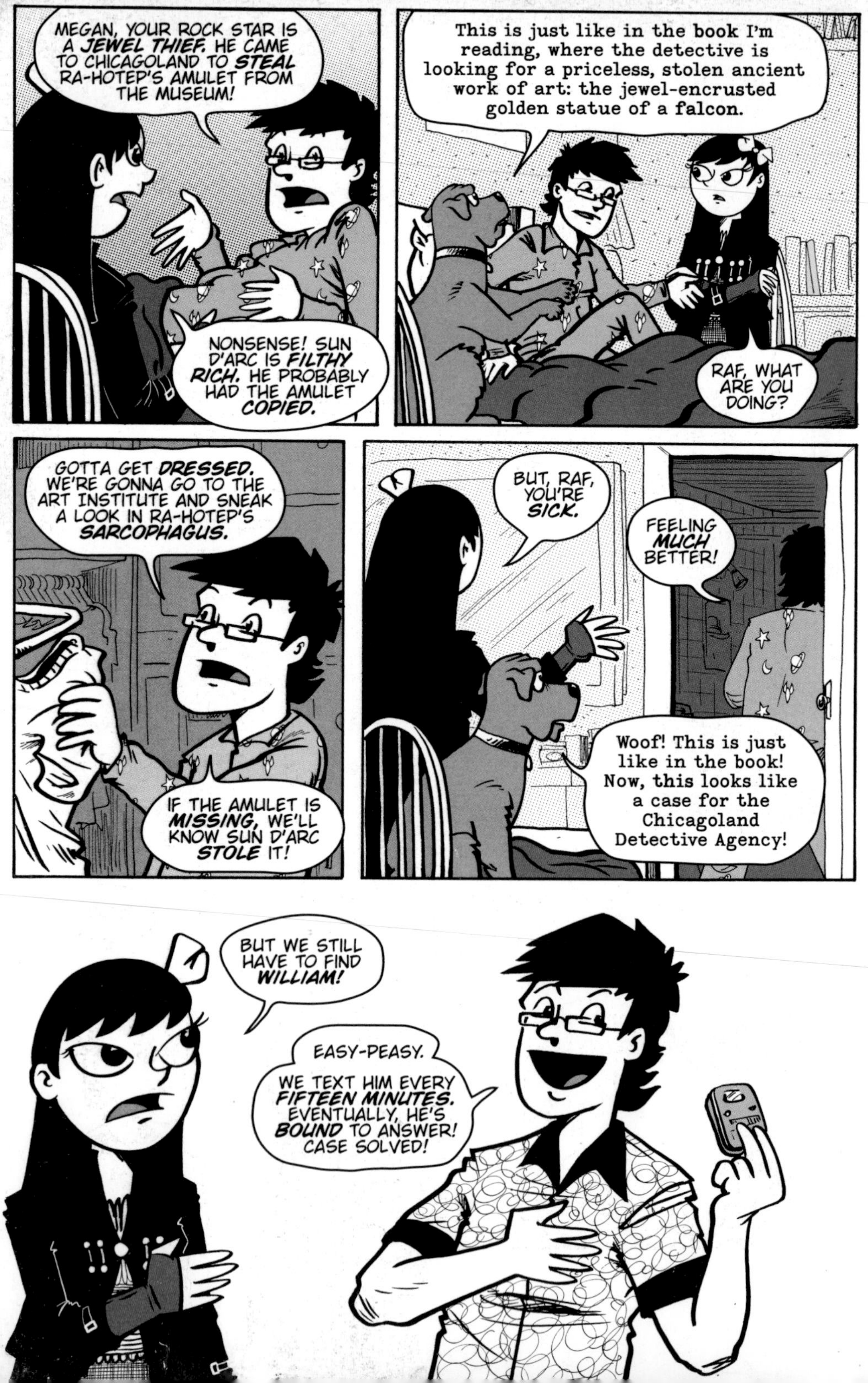
MEGAN, YOUR ROCK STAR IS A JEWEL THIEF. HE CAME TO CHICAGOLAND TO STEAL RA-HOTEP'S AMULET FROM THE MUSEUM!
NONSENSE! SUN D'ARC IS FILTHY RICH. HE PROBABLY HAD THE AMULET COPIED.
This is just like in the book I'm reading, where the detective is looking for a priceless, stolen ancient work of art: the jewel-encrusted golden statue of a falcon.
RAF, WHAT ARE YOU DOING?
GOTTA GET DRESSED. WE'RE GONNA GO TO THE ART INSTITUTE AND SNEAK A LOOK IN RA-HOTEP'S SARCOPHAGUS.
IF THE AMULET IS MISSING, WE'LL KNOW SUN D'ARC STOLE IT!
BUT, RAF, YOU'RE SICK.
FEELING MUCH BETTER!
Woof! This is just like in the book! Now, this looks like a case for the Chicagoland Detective Agency!
BUT WE STILL HAVE TO FIND WILLIAM!
EASY-PEASY.
WE TEXT HIM EVERY FIFTEEN MINUTES. EVENTUALLY, HE'S BOUND TO ANSWER! CASE SOLVED!

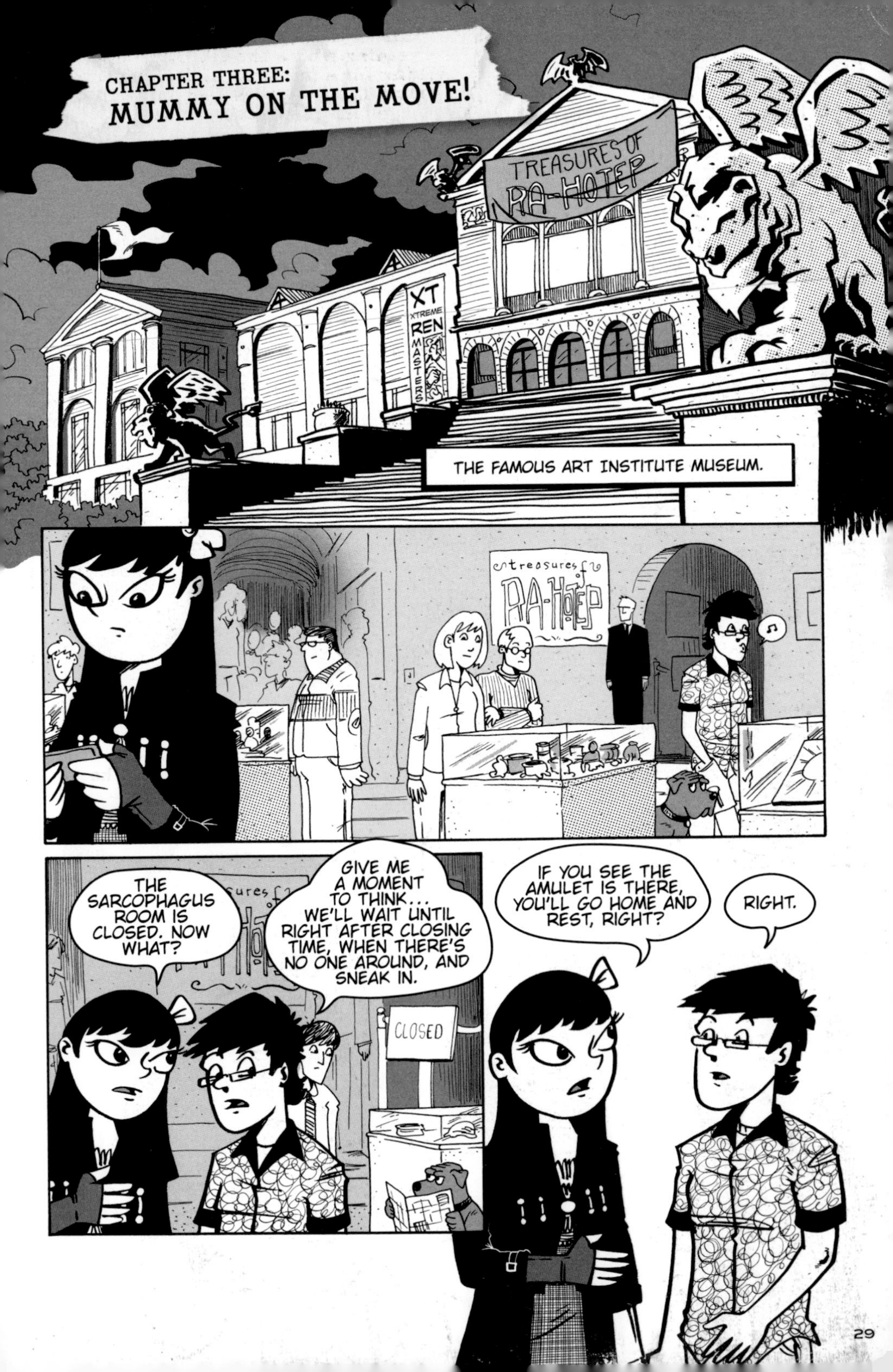
CHAPTER THREE:
MUMMY ON THE MOVE!
TREASURES OF RA-HOTEP
XT XTREME REN MASTERS
THE FAMOUS ART INSTITUTE MUSEUM.
treasures of RA-HOTEP
THE SARCOPHAGUS ROOM IS CLOSED. NOW WHAT?
GIVE ME A MOMENT TO THINK... WE'LL WAIT UNTIL RIGHT AFTER CLOSING TIME, WHEN THERE'S NO ONE AROUND, AND SNEAK IN.
CLOSED
IF YOU SEE THE AMULET IS THERE, YOU'LL GO HOME AND REST, RIGHT?
RIGHT.

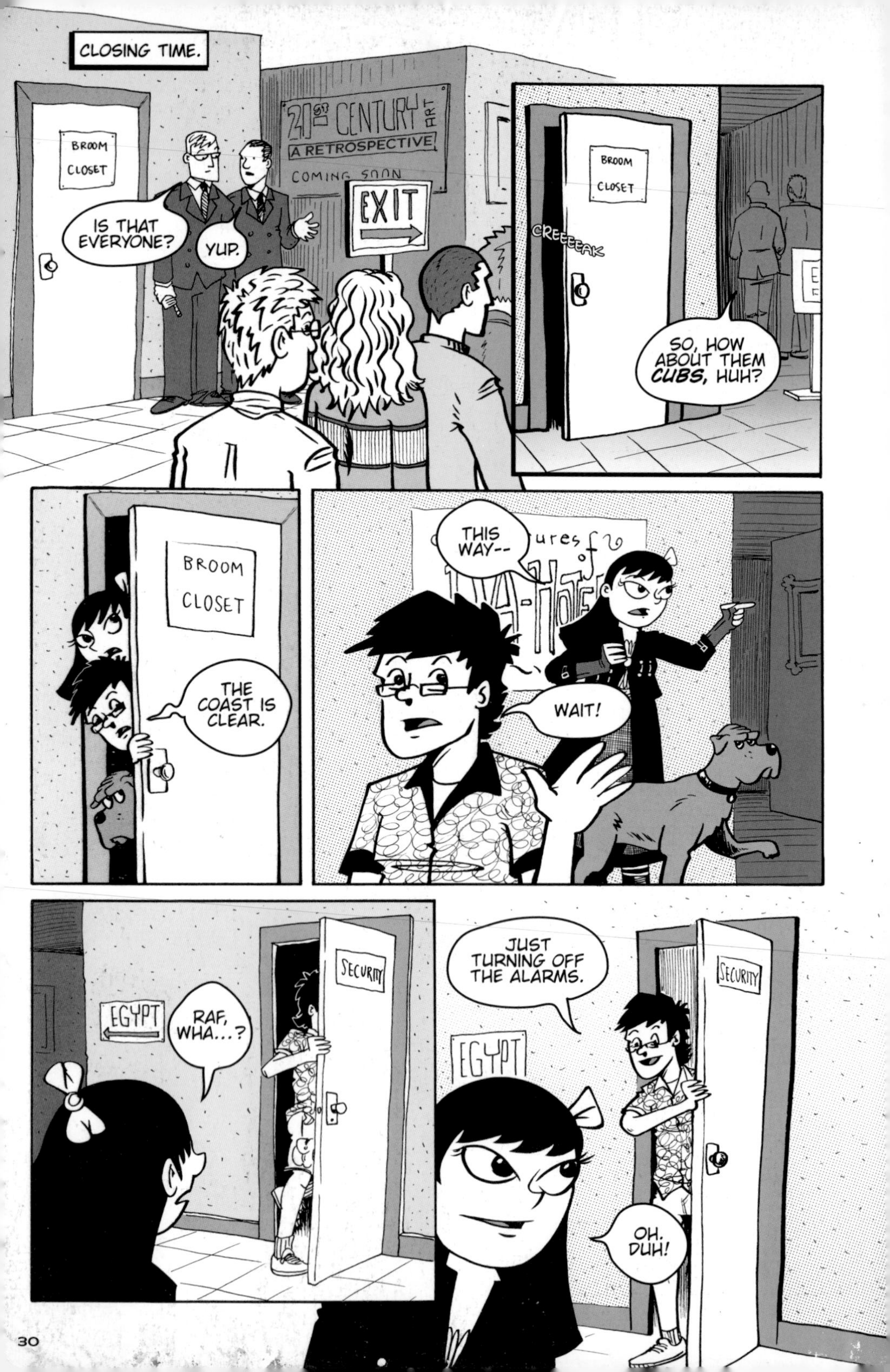
CLOSING TIME.
BROOM CLOSET
20th CENTURY ART
A RETROSPECTIVE
COMING SOON
EXIT
IS THAT EVERYONE?
YUP.
BROOM CLOSET
CREEEEAK
SO, HOW ABOUT THEM CUBS, HUH?
BROOM CLOSET
THE COAST IS CLEAR.
THIS WAY--
WAIT!
EGYPT
SECURITY
RAF, WHA...?
JUST TURNING OFF THE ALARMS.
SECURITY
EGYPT
OH. DUH!

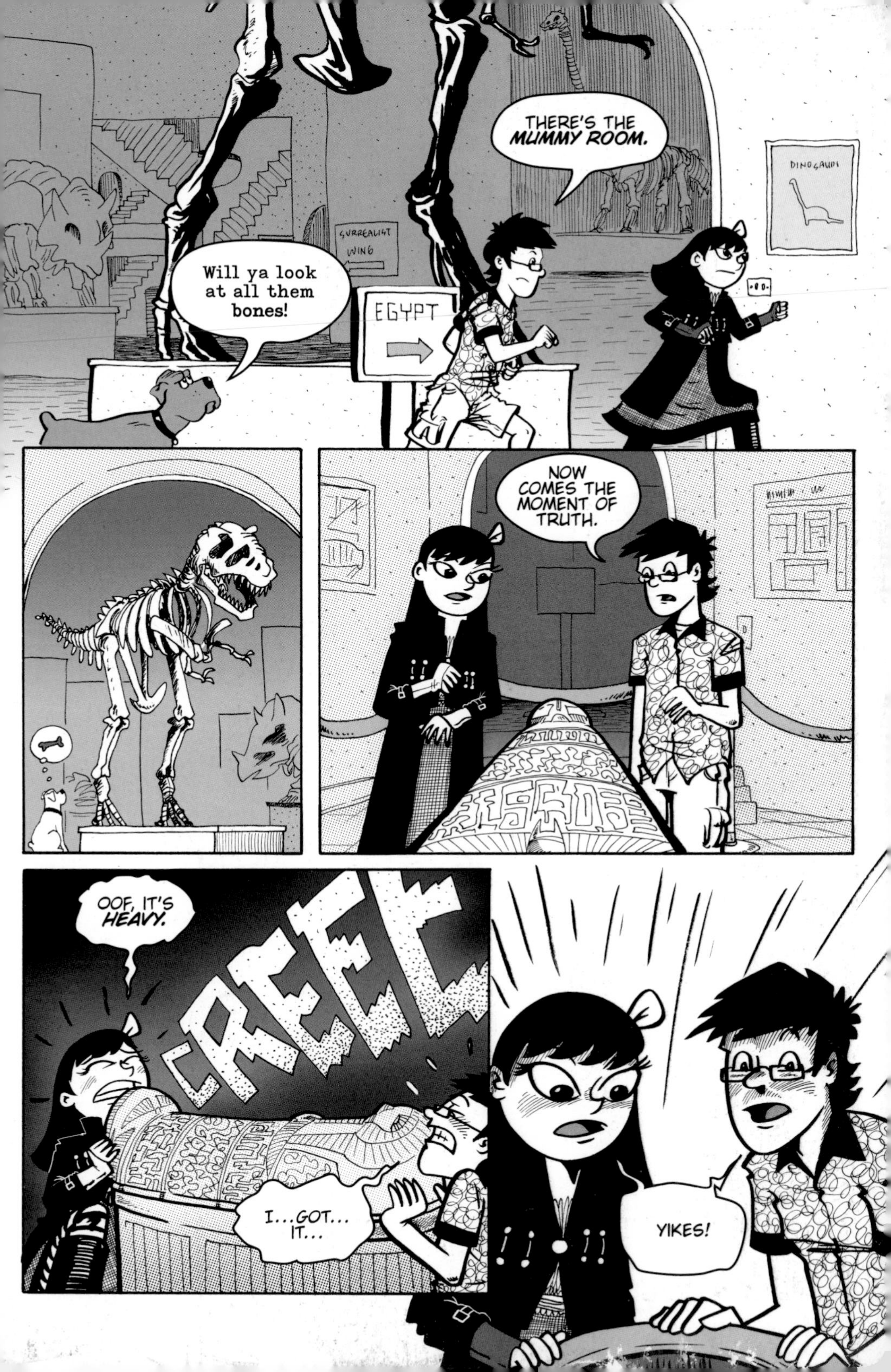
THERE'S THE *MUMMY ROOM.*
SURREALIST WING
Will ya look at all them bones!
EGYPT
DINOSAURS
NOW COMES THE MOMENT OF TRUTH.
OOF, IT'S *HEAVY.*
CREEE
I...GOT... IT...
YIKES!

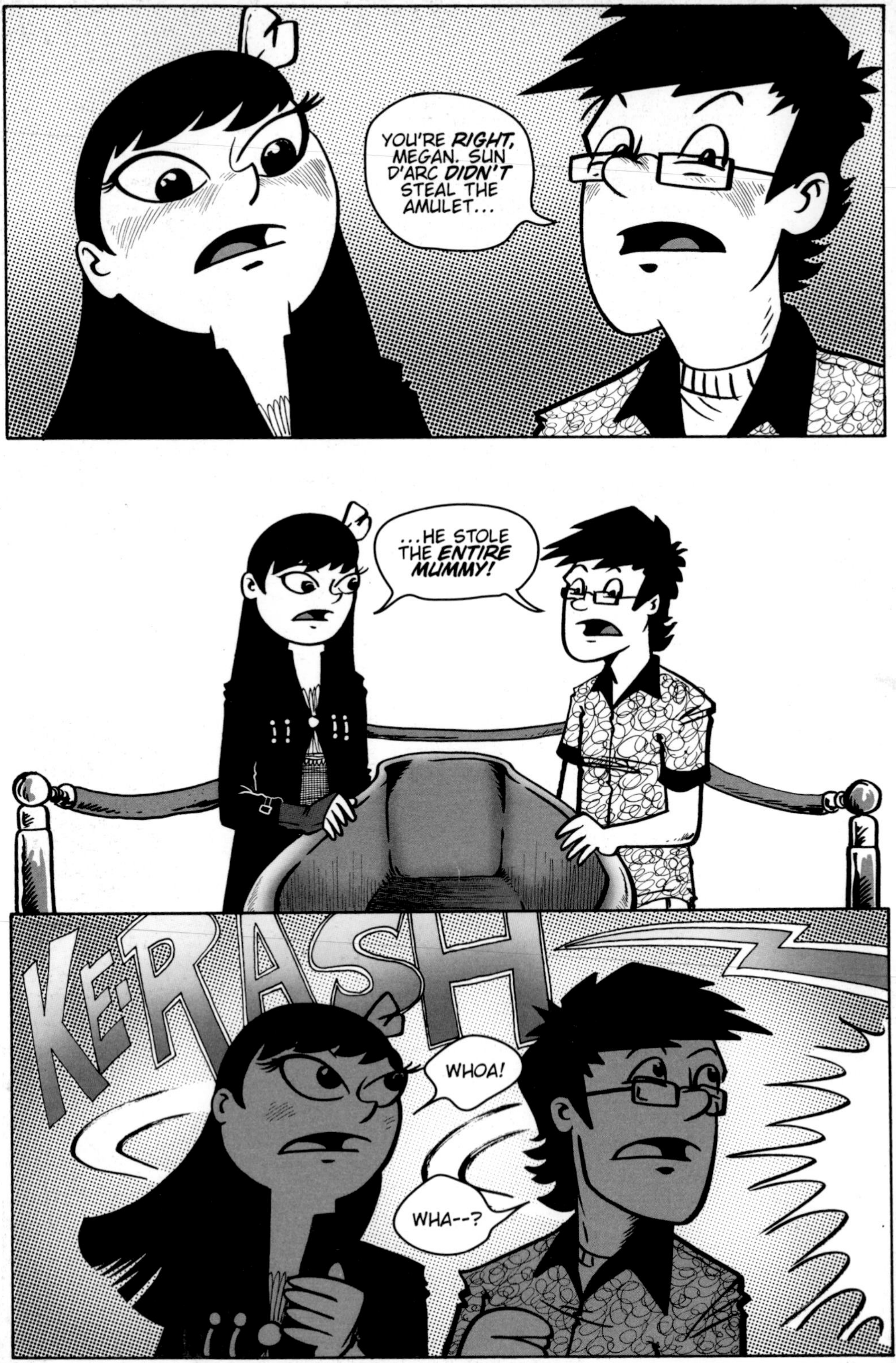
YOU'RE RIGHT, MEGAN. SUN D'ARC DIDN'T STEAL THE AMULET...
...HE STOLE THE ENTIRE MUMMY!
KE-RASH
WHOA!
WHA--?

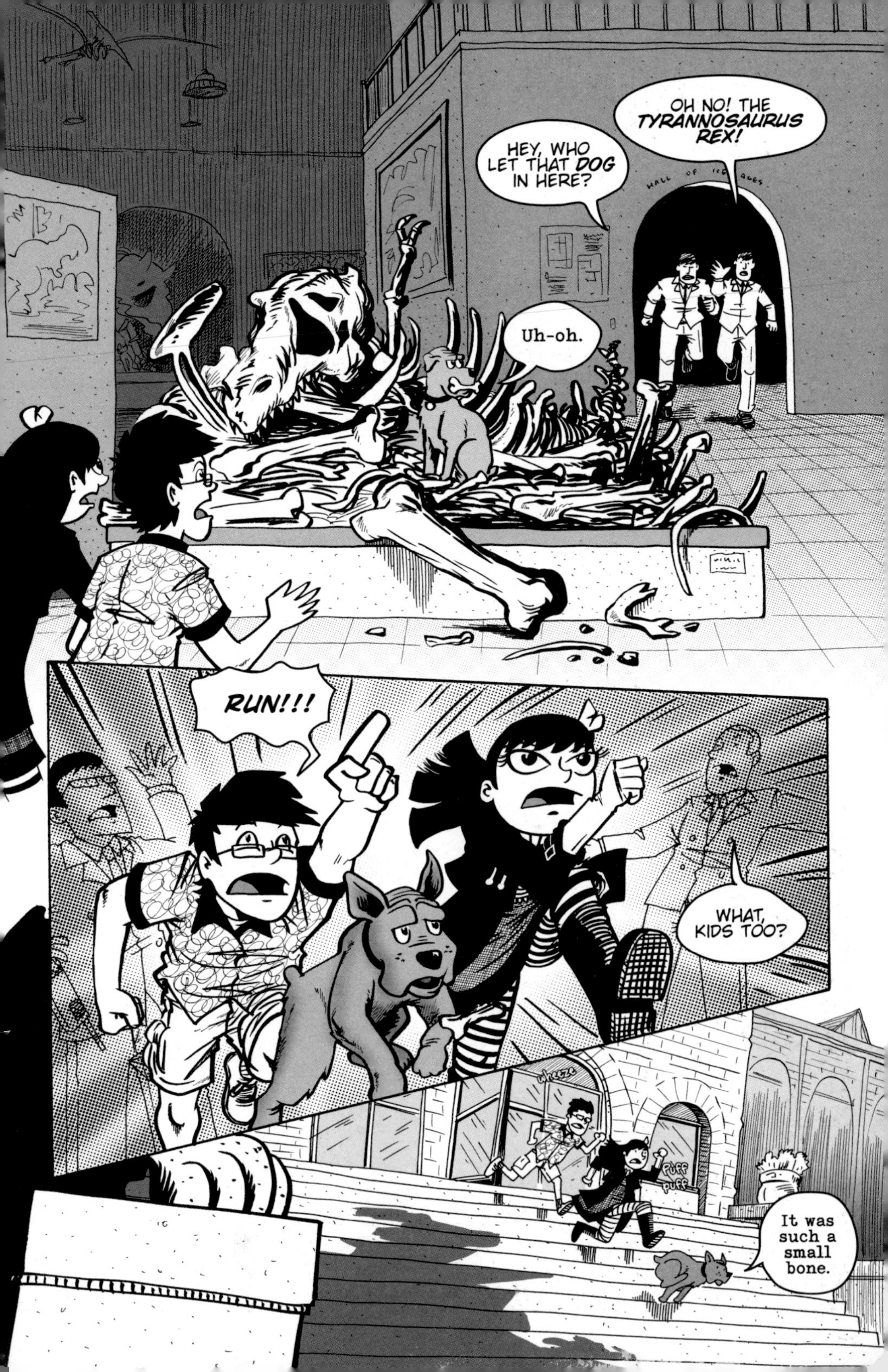
HEY, WHO LET THAT DOG IN HERE?
OH NO! THE TYRANNOSAURUS REX!
HALL OF ICE AGES
Uh-oh.
RUN!!!
WHAT, KIDS TOO?
PUFF PUFF
It was such a small bone.

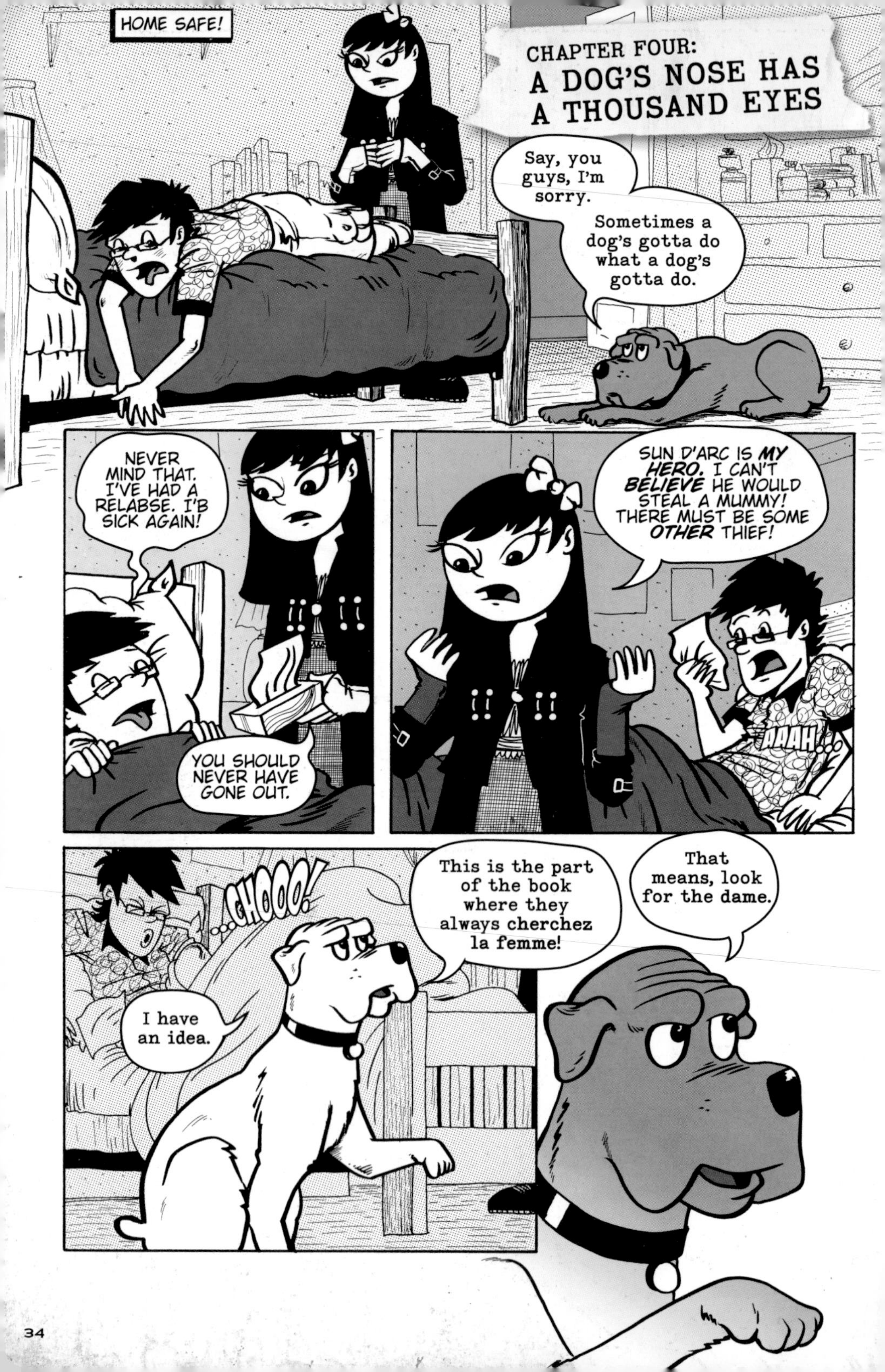
HOME SAFE!
CHAPTER FOUR: A DOG'S NOSE HAS A THOUSAND EYES
Say, you guys, I'm sorry.
Sometimes a dog's gotta do what a dog's gotta do.
NEVER MIND THAT. I'VE HAD A RELABSE. I'B SICK AGAIN!
YOU SHOULD NEVER HAVE GONE OUT.
SUN D'ARC IS MY HERO. I CAN'T BELIEVE HE WOULD STEAL A MUMMY! THERE MUST BE SOME OTHER THIEF!
AAAH...
...CHOOO!
I have an idea.
This is the part of the book where they always cherchez la femme!
That means, look for the dame.

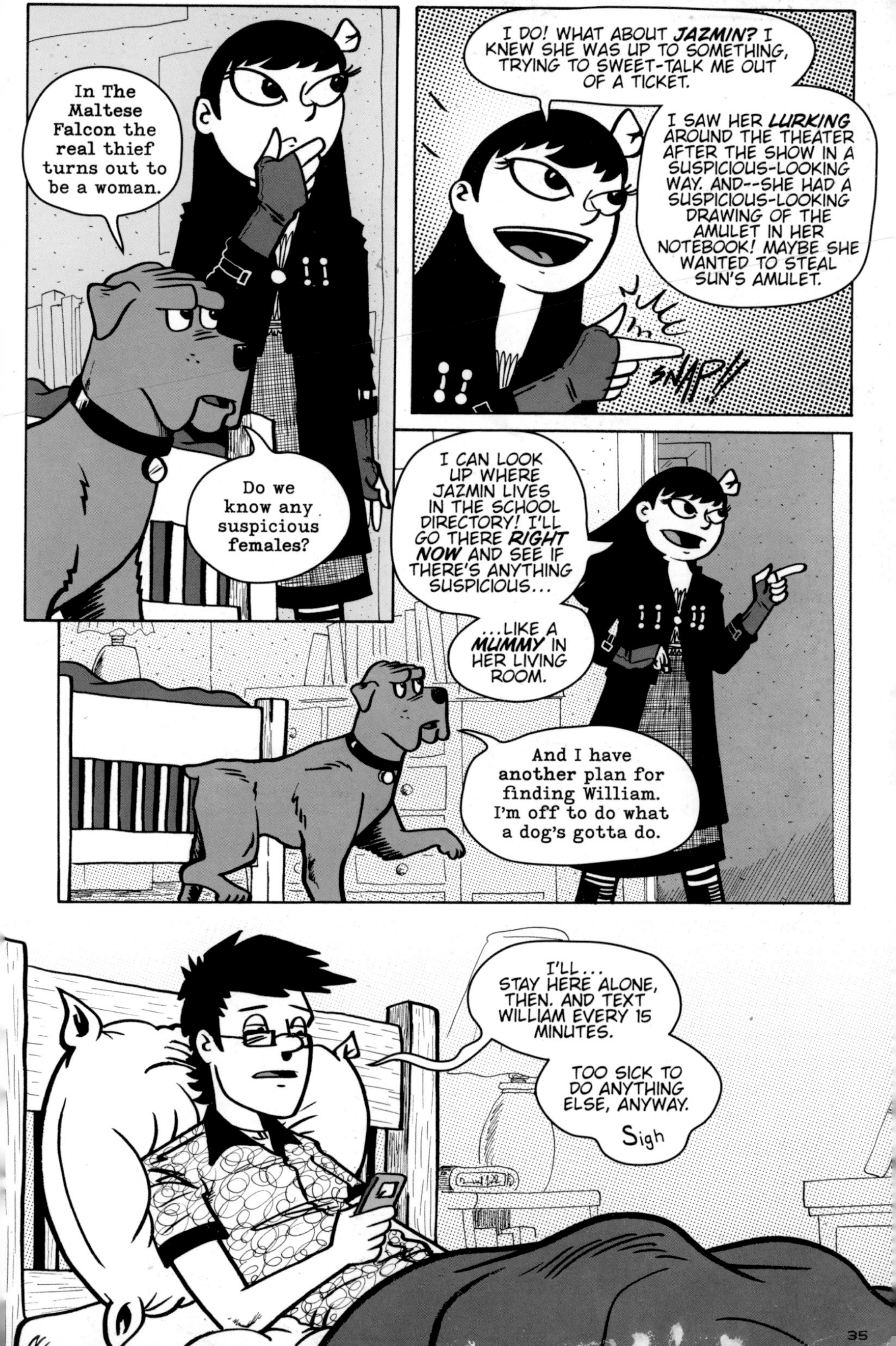
In The Maltese Falcon the real thief turns out to be a woman.
Do we know any suspicious females?
I DO! WHAT ABOUT JAZMIN? I KNEW SHE WAS UP TO SOMETHING, TRYING TO SWEET-TALK ME OUT OF A TICKET.
I SAW HER LURKING AROUND THE THEATER AFTER THE SHOW IN A SUSPICIOUS-LOOKING WAY. AND--SHE HAD A SUSPICIOUS-LOOKING DRAWING OF THE AMULET IN HER NOTEBOOK! MAYBE SHE WANTED TO STEAL SUN'S AMULET.
SNAP!!
I CAN LOOK UP WHERE JAZMIN LIVES IN THE SCHOOL DIRECTORY! I'LL GO THERE RIGHT NOW AND SEE IF THERE'S ANYTHING SUSPICIOUS...
...LIKE A MUMMY IN HER LIVING ROOM.
And I have another plan for finding William. I'm off to do what a dog's gotta do.
I'LL... STAY HERE ALONE, THEN. AND TEXT WILLIAM EVERY 15 MINUTES.
TOO SICK TO DO ANYTHING ELSE, ANYWAY.
Sigh

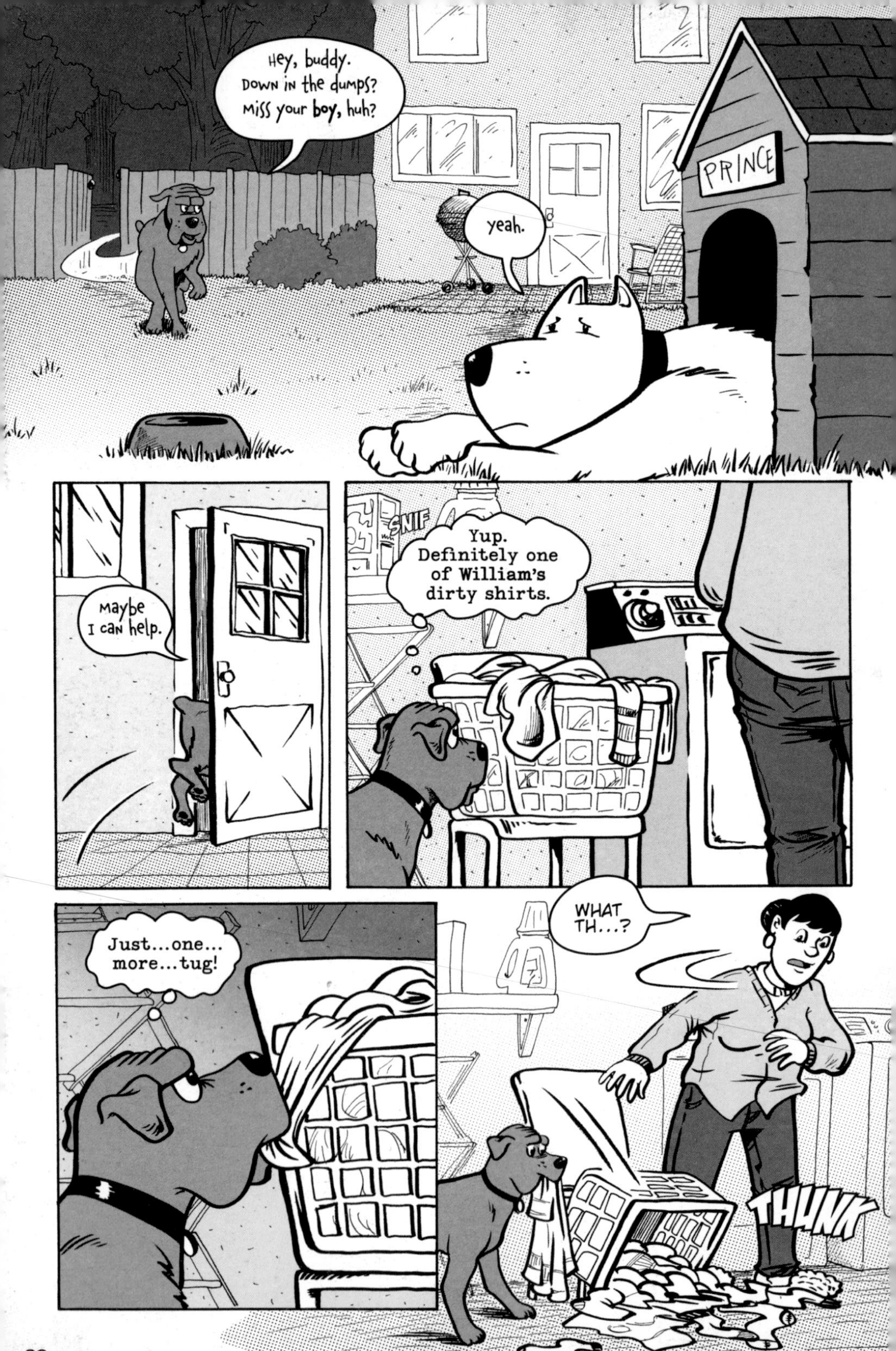
Hey, buddy.
Down in the dumps?
Miss your boy, huh?
yeah.
PRINCE
Maybe
I can help.
SNIF
Yup.
Definitely one
of William's
dirty shirts.
Just...one...
more...tug!
WHAT
TH...?
THUNK

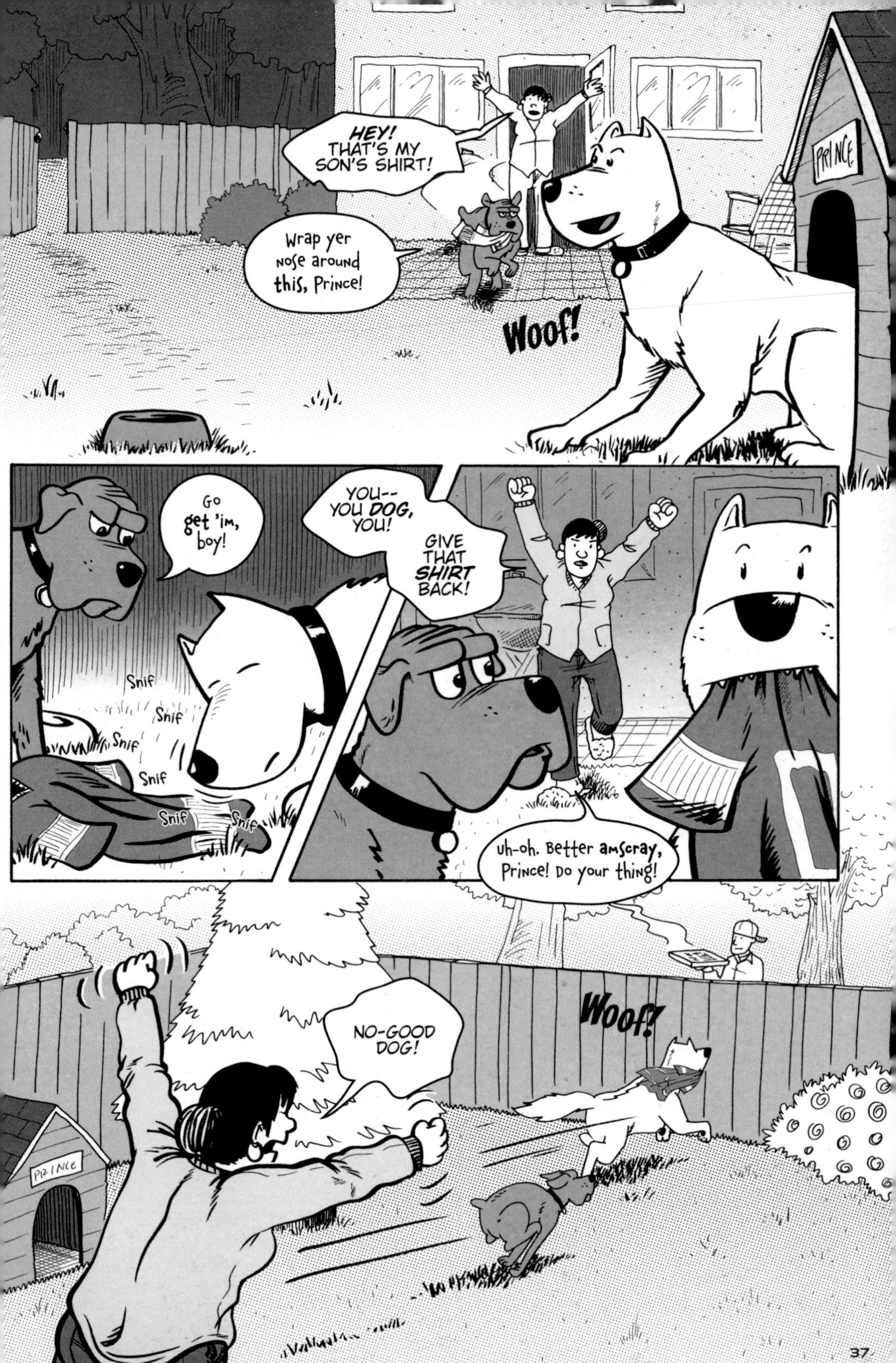
HEY! THAT'S MY SON'S SHIRT!
Wrap yer nose around this, Prince!
PRINCE
Woof!
Go get 'im, boy!
Snif
Snif
Snif
Snif
Snif
Snif
YOU-- YOU DOG, YOU!
GIVE THAT SHIRT BACK!
uh-oh. Better amscray, Prince! Do your thing!
NO-GOOD DOG!
Woof!
PRINCE

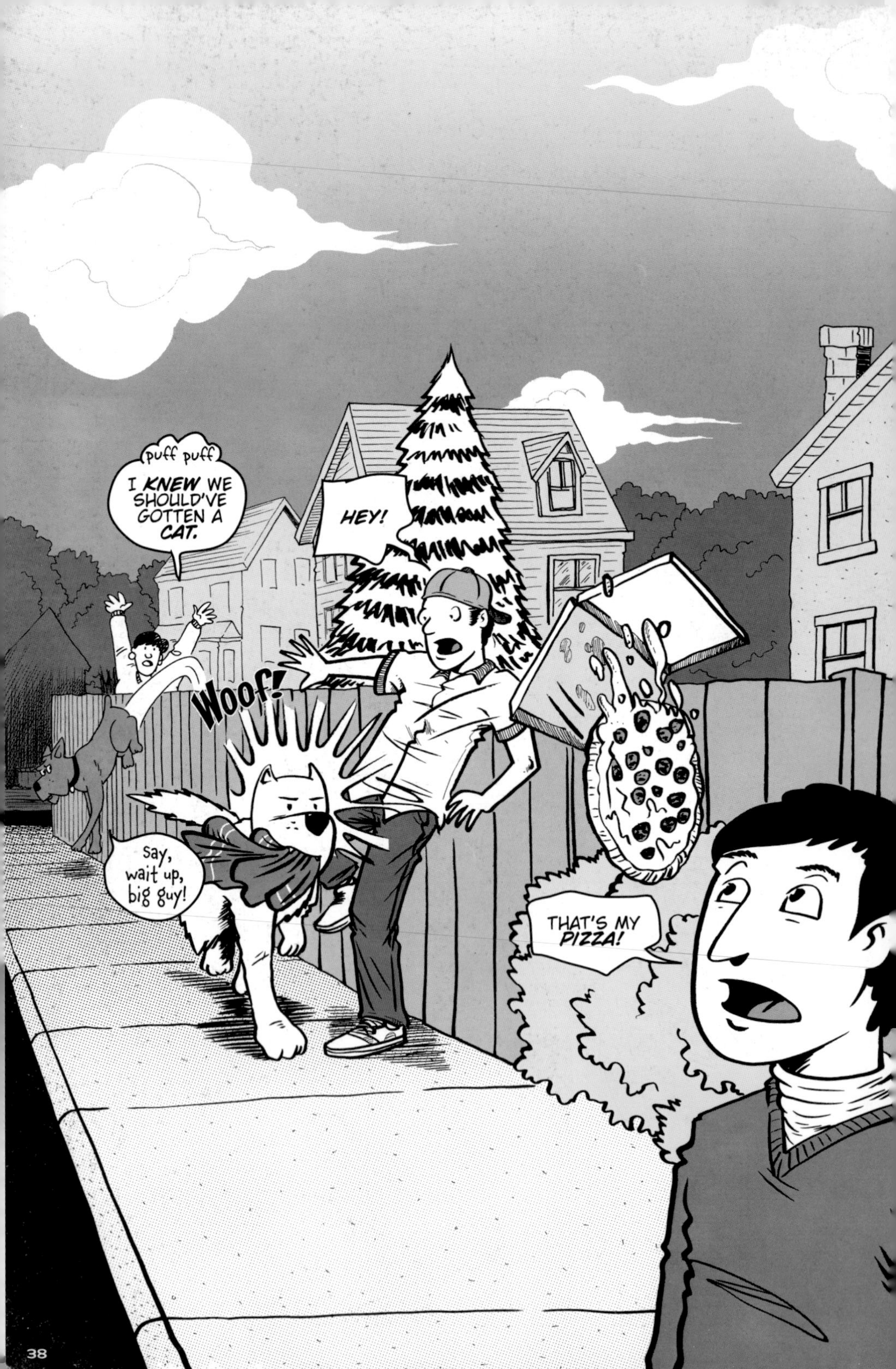
puff puff
I KNEW WE SHOULD'VE GOTTEN A CAT.
HEY!
Woof!
say, wait up, big guy!
THAT'S MY PIZZA!

CHAPTER FIVE: ON DANGEROUS GROUND

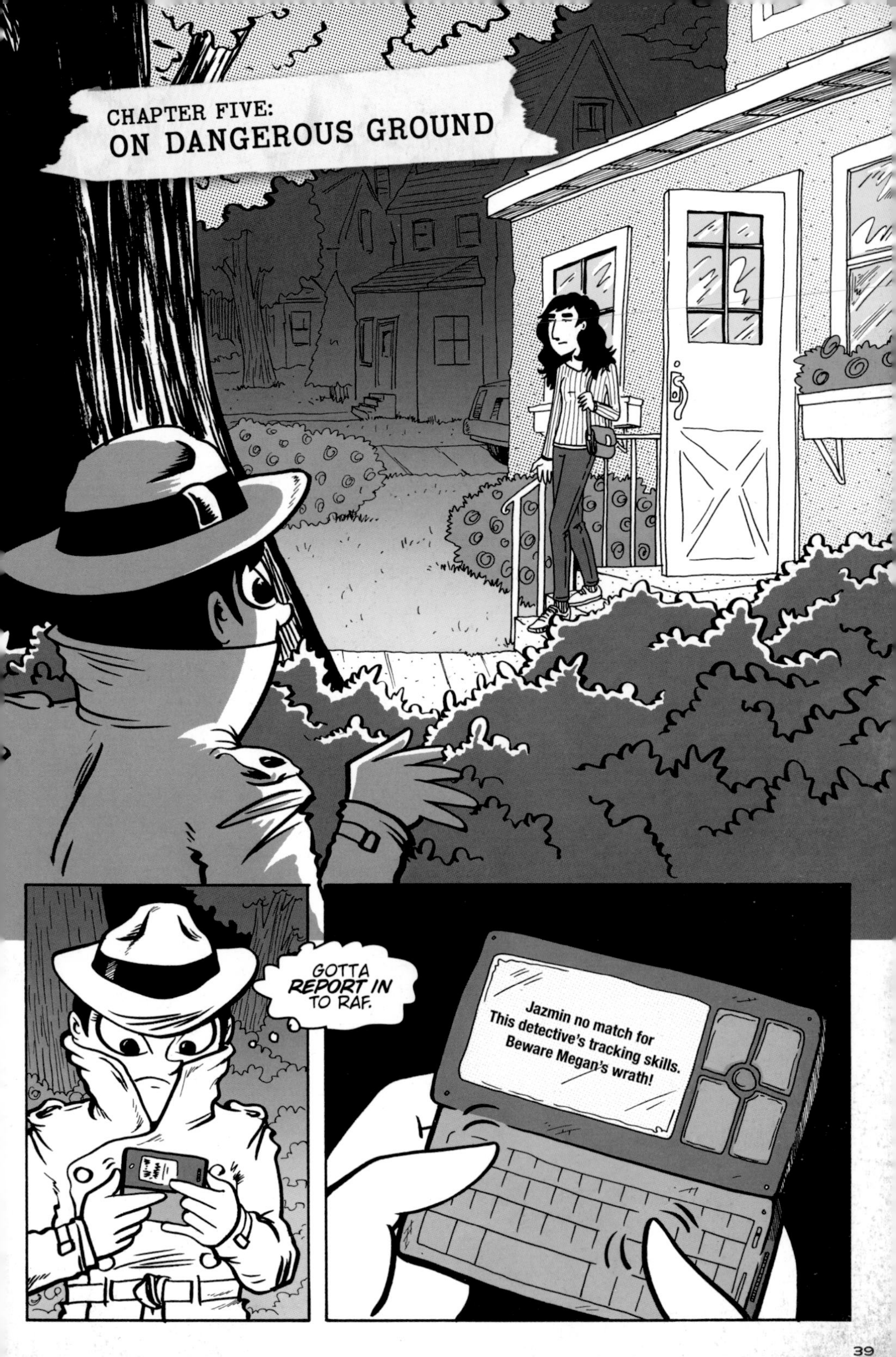
GOTTA REPORT IN TO RAF.
Jazmin no match for
This detective's tracking skills.
Beware Megan's wrath!

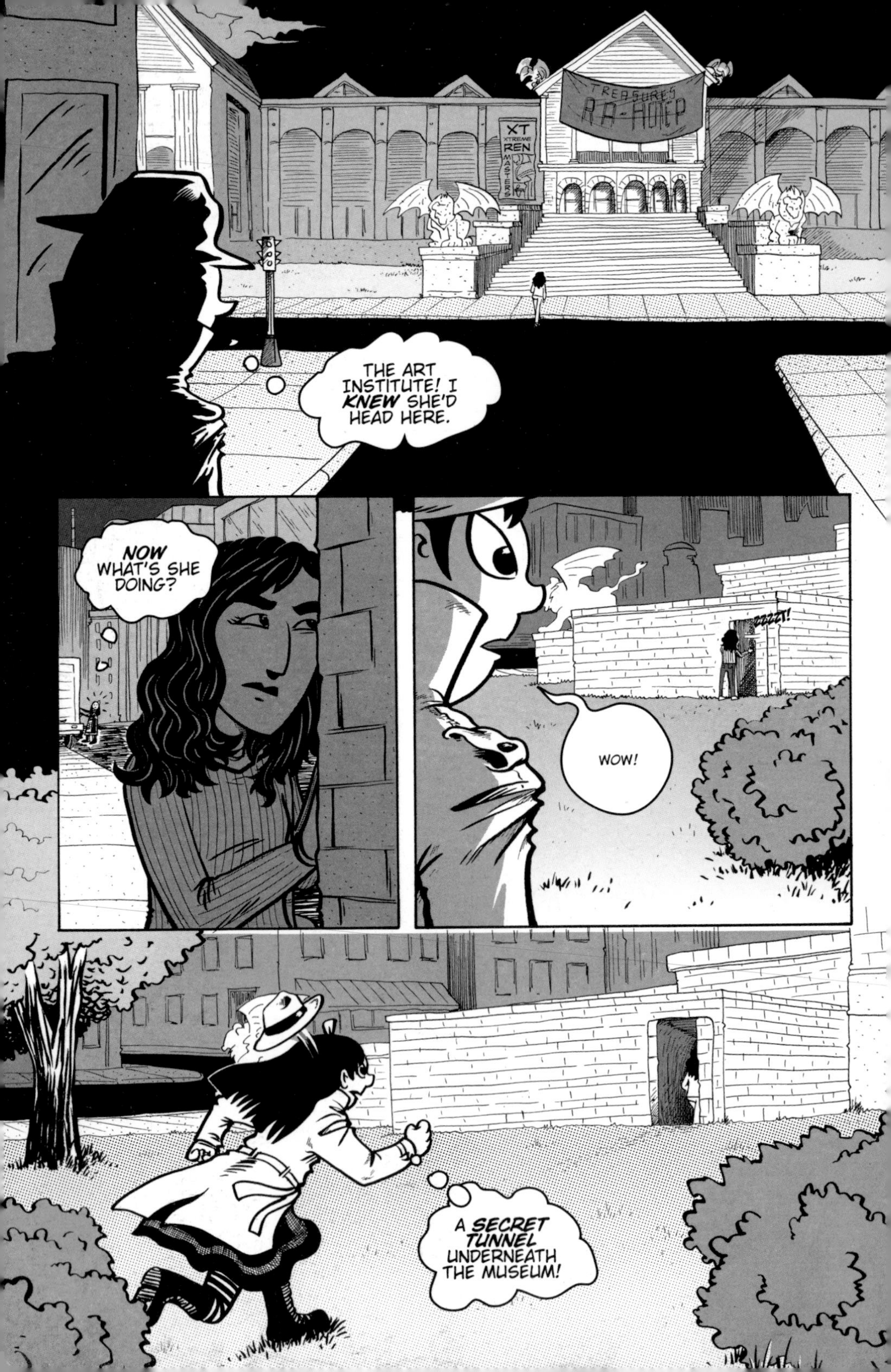
TREASURES RA-HOTEP
XT XTREME REN MASTERS
THE ART INSTITUTE! I *KNEW* SHE'D HEAD HERE.
NOW WHAT'S SHE DOING?
ZZZZZT!
WOW!
A *SECRET TUNNEL* UNDERNEATH THE MUSEUM!

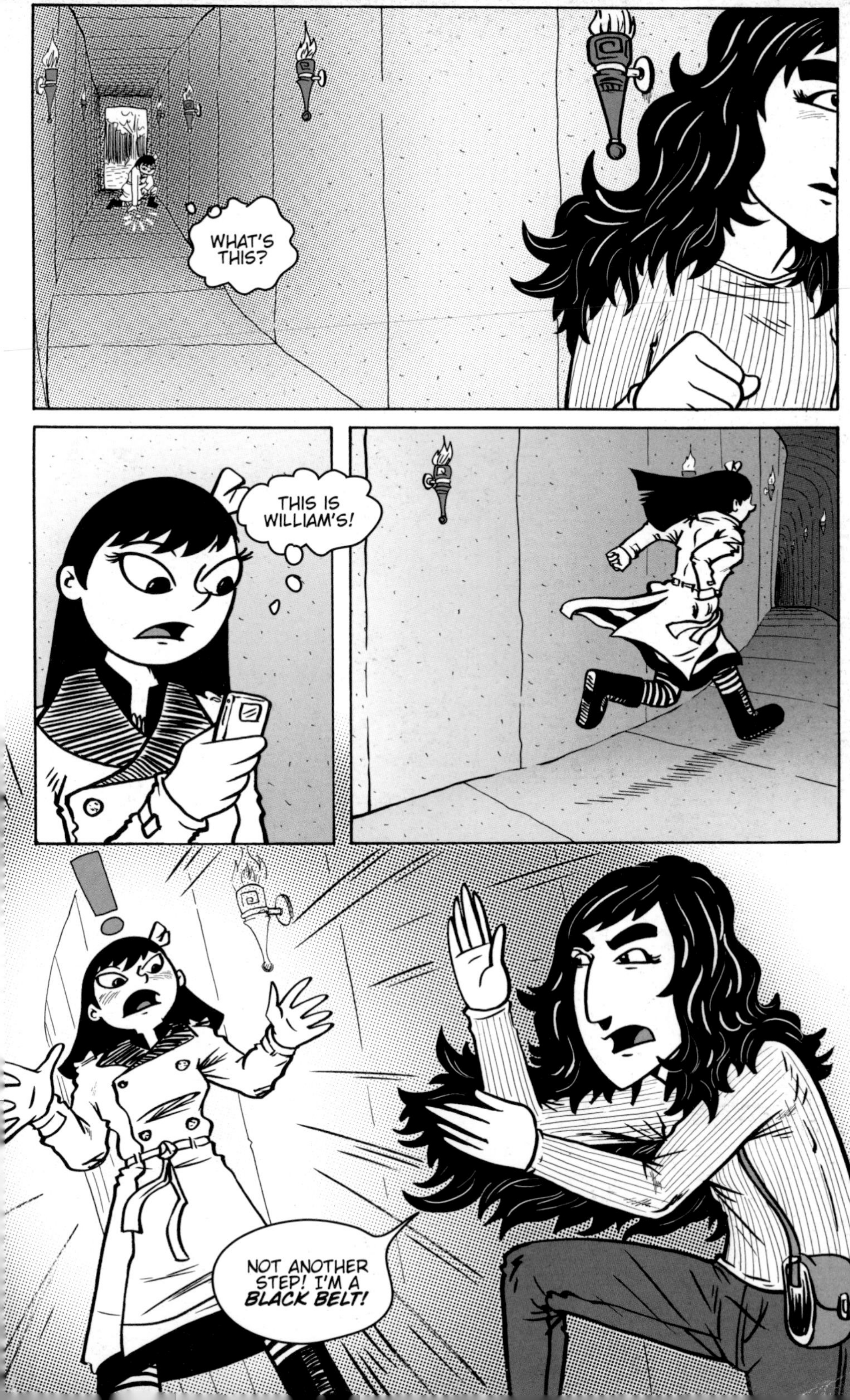
WHAT'S THIS?
THIS IS WILLIAM'S!
!
NOT ANOTHER STEP! I'M A ***BLACK BELT!***

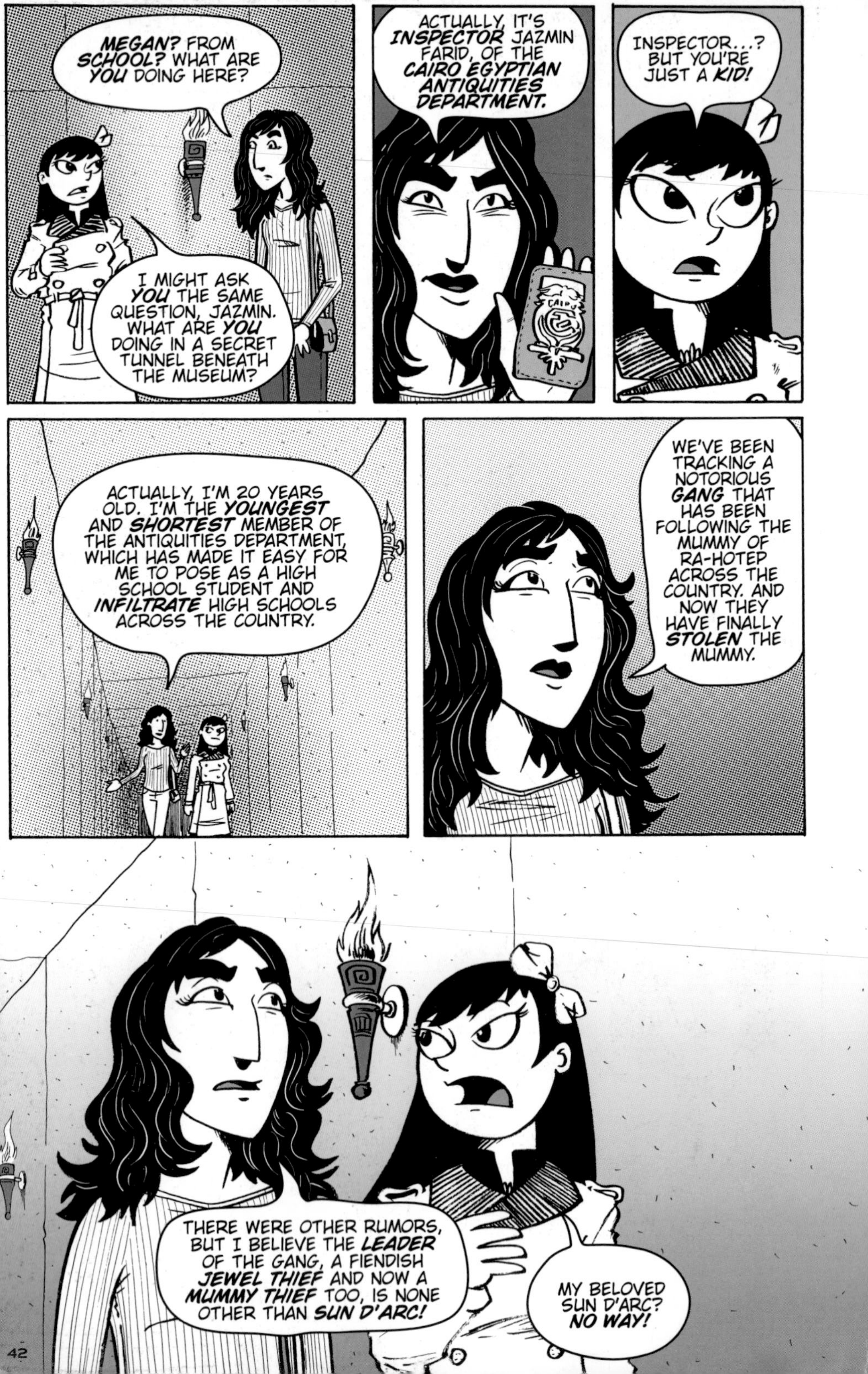
MEGAN? FROM SCHOOL? WHAT ARE YOU DOING HERE?
I MIGHT ASK YOU THE SAME QUESTION, JAZMIN. WHAT ARE YOU DOING IN A SECRET TUNNEL BENEATH THE MUSEUM?
ACTUALLY, IT'S INSPECTOR JAZMIN FARID, OF THE CAIRO EGYPTIAN ANTIQUITIES DEPARTMENT.
CAIRO
INSPECTOR...? BUT YOU'RE JUST A KID!
ACTUALLY, I'M 20 YEARS OLD. I'M THE YOUNGEST AND SHORTEST MEMBER OF THE ANTIQUITIES DEPARTMENT, WHICH HAS MADE IT EASY FOR ME TO POSE AS A HIGH SCHOOL STUDENT AND INFILTRATE HIGH SCHOOLS ACROSS THE COUNTRY.
WE'VE BEEN TRACKING A NOTORIOUS GANG THAT HAS BEEN FOLLOWING THE MUMMY OF RA-HOTEP ACROSS THE COUNTRY. AND NOW THEY HAVE FINALLY STOLEN THE MUMMY.
THERE WERE OTHER RUMORS, BUT I BELIEVE THE LEADER OF THE GANG, A FIENDISH JEWEL THIEF AND NOW A MUMMY THIEF TOO, IS NONE OTHER THAN SUN D'ARC!
MY BELOVED SUN D'ARC? NO WAY!

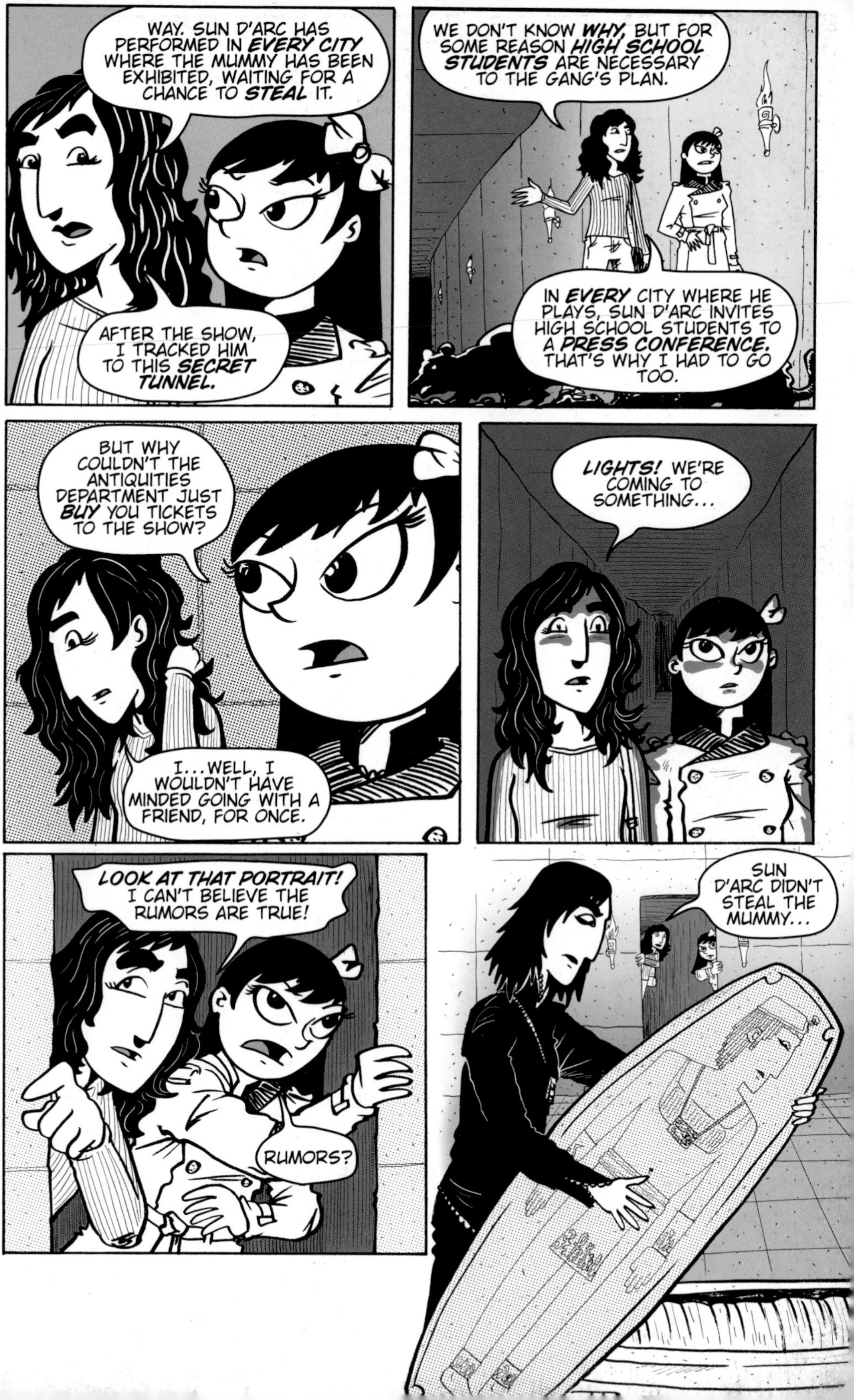
WAY. SUN D'ARC HAS PERFORMED IN EVERY CITY WHERE THE MUMMY HAS BEEN EXHIBITED, WAITING FOR A CHANCE TO STEAL IT.
AFTER THE SHOW, I TRACKED HIM TO THIS SECRET TUNNEL.
WE DON'T KNOW WHY, BUT FOR SOME REASON HIGH SCHOOL STUDENTS ARE NECESSARY TO THE GANG'S PLAN.
IN EVERY CITY WHERE HE PLAYS, SUN D'ARC INVITES HIGH SCHOOL STUDENTS TO A PRESS CONFERENCE. THAT'S WHY I HAD TO GO TOO.
BUT WHY COULDN'T THE ANTIQUITIES DEPARTMENT JUST BUY YOU TICKETS TO THE SHOW?
I...WELL, I WOULDN'T HAVE MINDED GOING WITH A FRIEND, FOR ONCE.
LIGHTS! WE'RE COMING TO SOMETHING...
LOOK AT THAT PORTRAIT! I CAN'T BELIEVE THE RUMORS ARE TRUE!
RUMORS?
SUN D'ARC DIDN'T STEAL THE MUMMY...

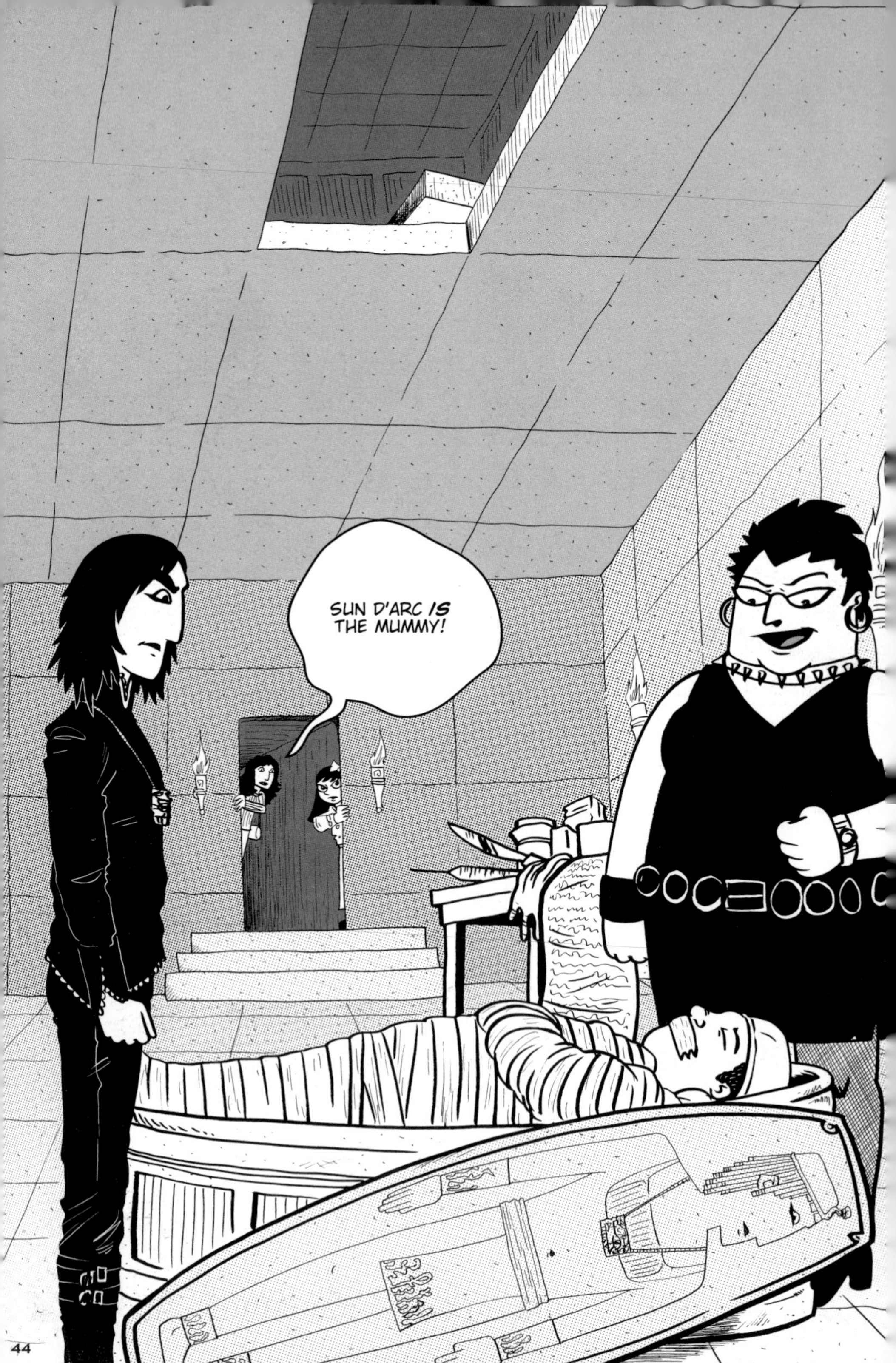
SUN D'ARC IS THE MUMMY!

CHAPTER SIX: DEADLINE AT MIDNIGHT

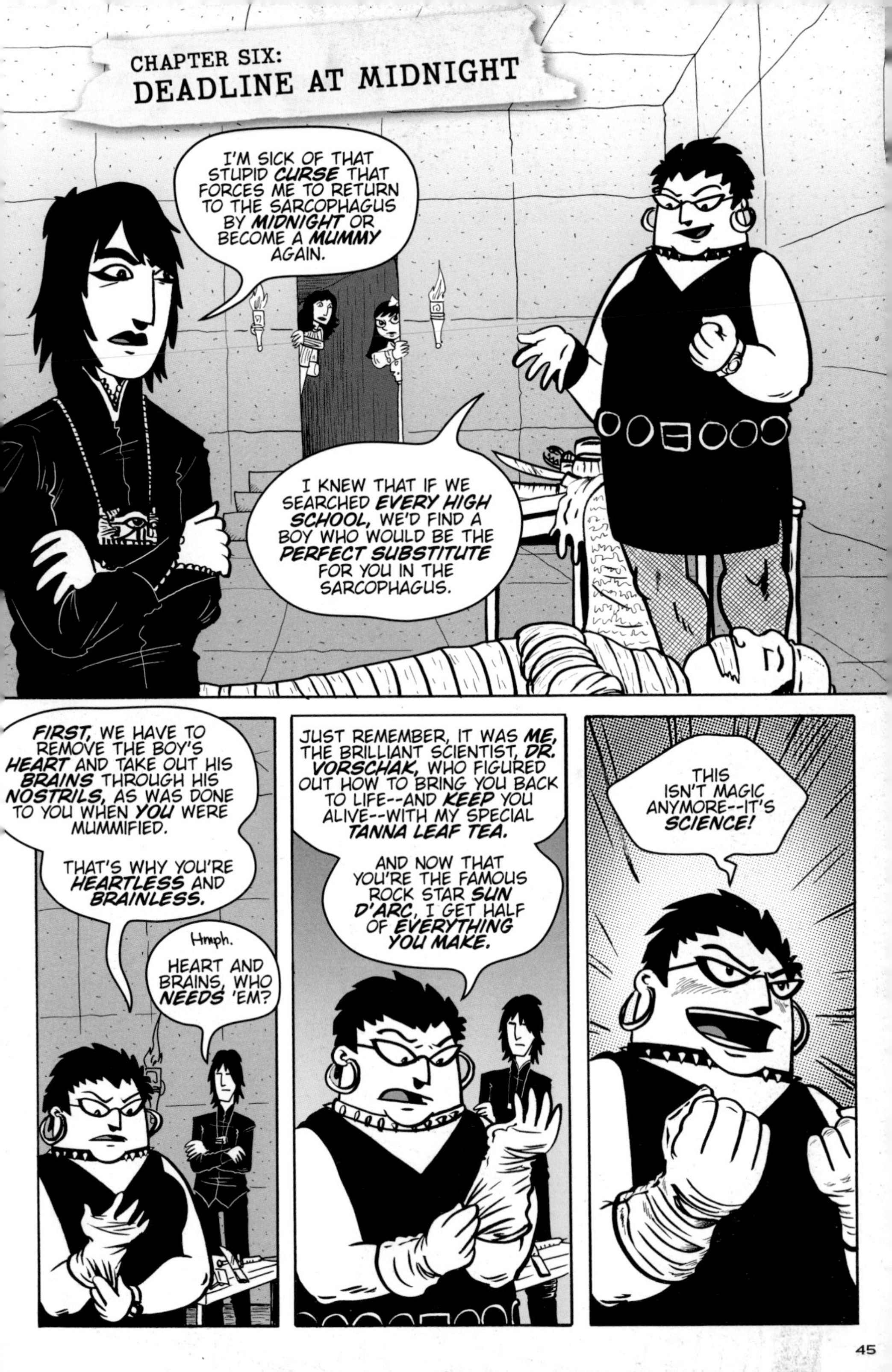

I'M SICK OF THAT STUPID CURSE THAT FORCES ME TO RETURN TO THE SARCOPHAGUS BY MIDNIGHT OR BECOME A MUMMY AGAIN.
I KNEW THAT IF WE SEARCHED EVERY HIGH SCHOOL, WE'D FIND A BOY WHO WOULD BE THE PERFECT SUBSTITUTE FOR YOU IN THE SARCOPHAGUS.
FIRST, WE HAVE TO REMOVE THE BOY'S HEART AND TAKE OUT HIS BRAINS THROUGH HIS NOSTRILS, AS WAS DONE TO YOU WHEN YOU WERE MUMMIFIED.
THAT'S WHY YOU'RE HEARTLESS AND BRAINLESS.
Hmph.
HEART AND BRAINS, WHO NEEDS 'EM?
JUST REMEMBER, IT WAS ME, THE BRILLIANT SCIENTIST, DR. VORSCHAK, WHO FIGURED OUT HOW TO BRING YOU BACK TO LIFE--AND KEEP YOU ALIVE--WITH MY SPECIAL TANNA LEAF TEA.
AND NOW THAT YOU'RE THE FAMOUS ROCK STAR SUN D'ARC, I GET HALF OF EVERYTHING YOU MAKE.
THIS ISN'T MAGIC ANYMORE--IT'S SCIENCE!

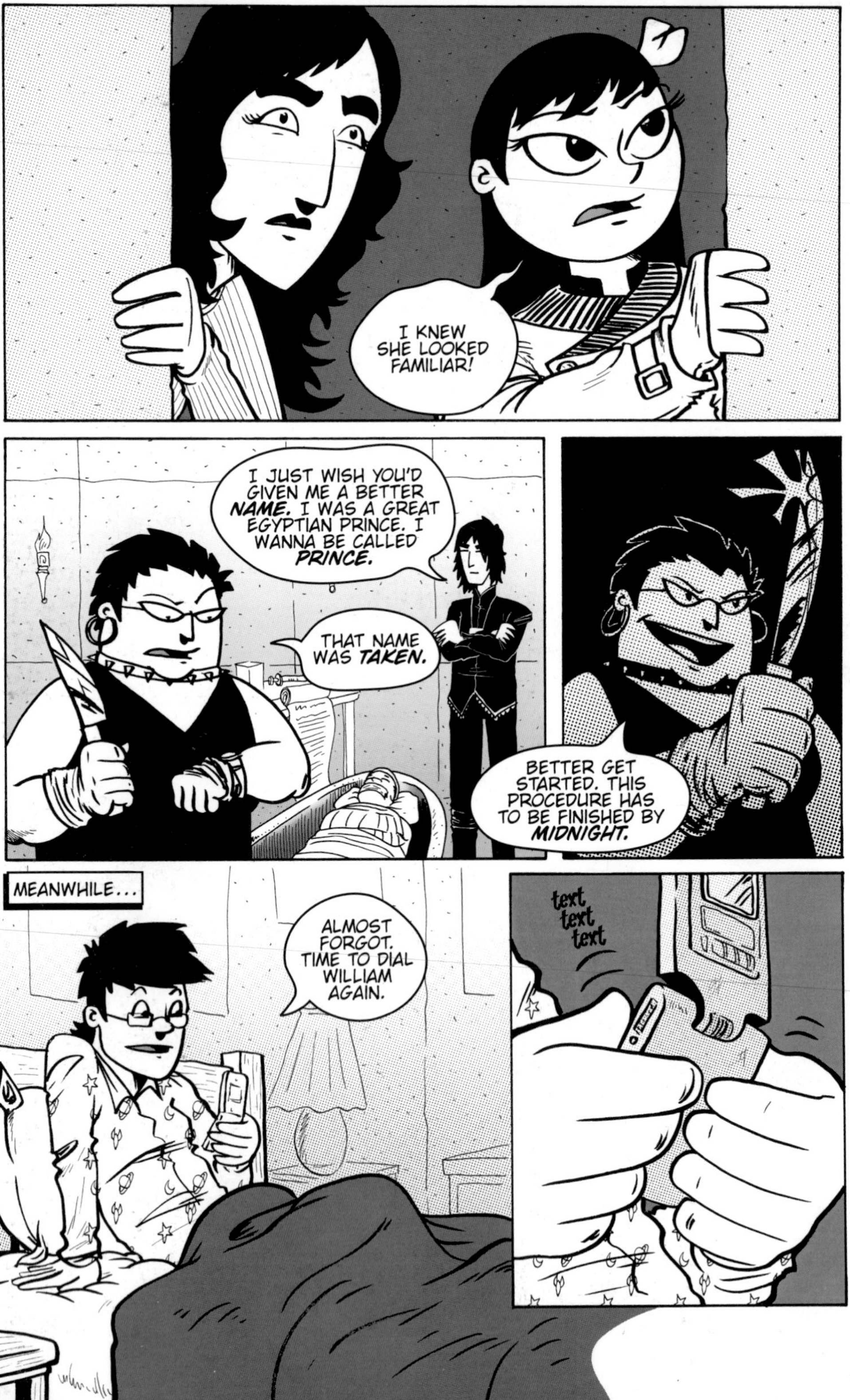
I KNEW SHE LOOKED FAMILIAR!
I JUST WISH YOU'D GIVEN ME A BETTER NAME. I WAS A GREAT EGYPTIAN PRINCE. I WANNA BE CALLED PRINCE.
THAT NAME WAS TAKEN.
BETTER GET STARTED. THIS PROCEDURE HAS TO BE FINISHED BY MIDNIGHT.
MEANWHILE...
ALMOST FORGOT. TIME TO DIAL WILLIAM AGAIN.
text text text

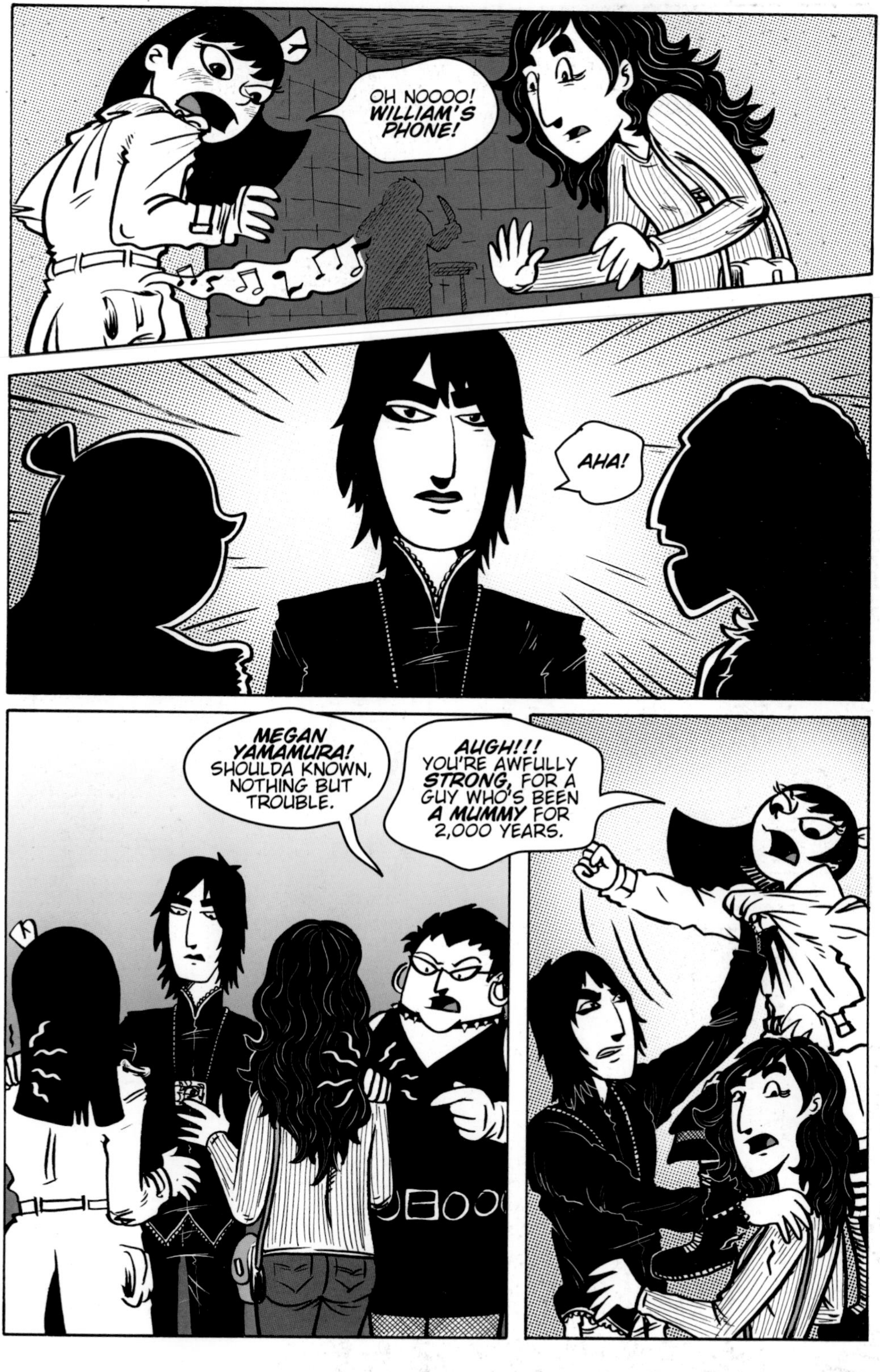
OH NOOOO! WILLIAM'S PHONE!
AHA!
MEGAN YAMAMURA! SHOULDA KNOWN, NOTHING BUT TROUBLE.
AUGH!!! YOU'RE AWFULLY STRONG, FOR A GUY WHO'S BEEN A MUMMY FOR 2,000 YEARS.

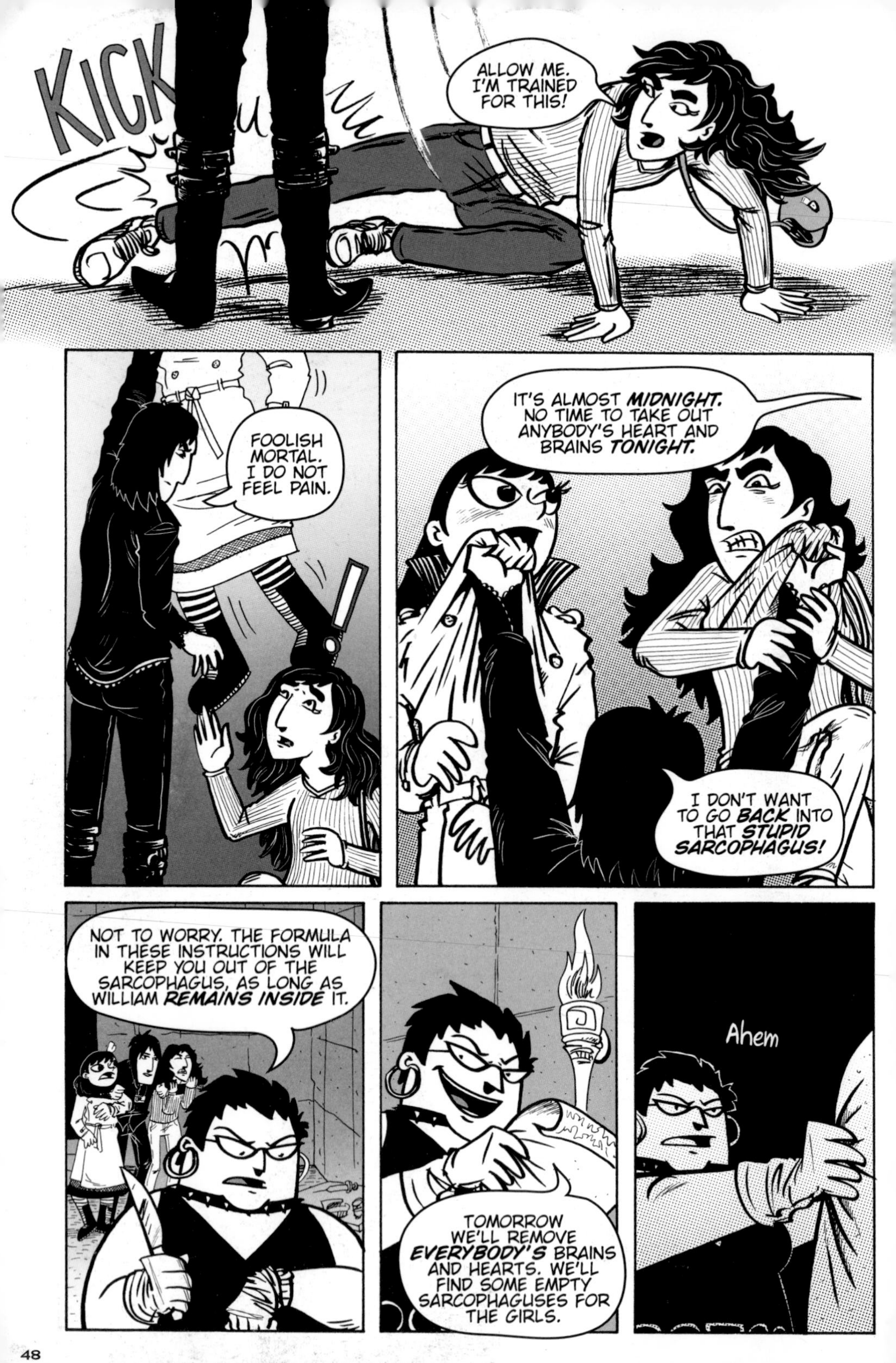
KICK
ALLOW ME. I'M TRAINED FOR THIS!
FOOLISH MORTAL. I DO NOT FEEL PAIN.
IT'S ALMOST MIDNIGHT. NO TIME TO TAKE OUT ANYBODY'S HEART AND BRAINS TONIGHT.
I DON'T WANT TO GO BACK INTO THAT STUPID SARCOPHAGUS!
NOT TO WORRY. THE FORMULA IN THESE INSTRUCTIONS WILL KEEP YOU OUT OF THE SARCOPHAGUS, AS LONG AS WILLIAM REMAINS INSIDE IT.
TOMORROW WE'LL REMOVE EVERYBODY'S BRAINS AND HEARTS. WE'LL FIND SOME EMPTY SARCOPHAGUSES FOR THE GIRLS.
Ahem

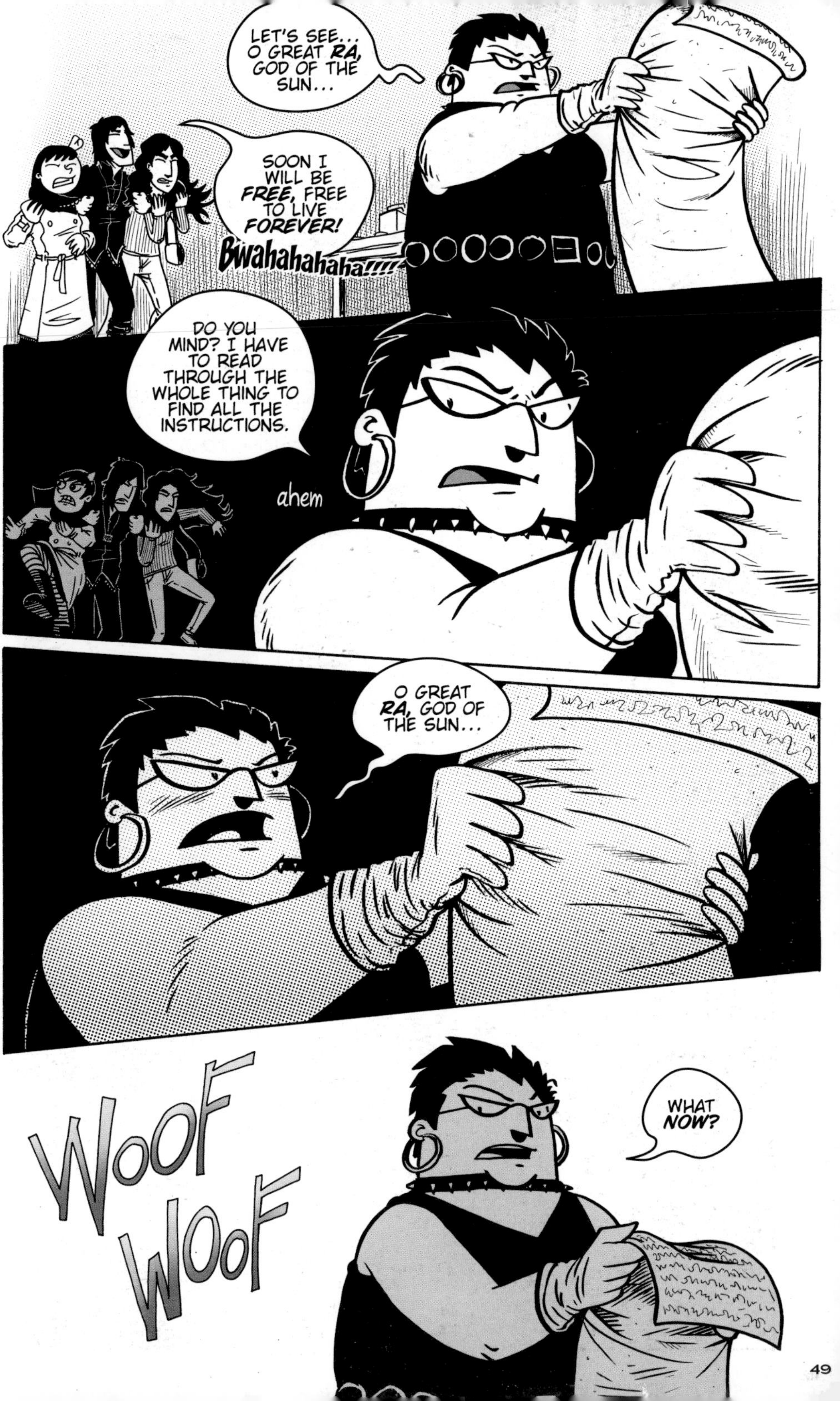
LET'S SEE... O GREAT **RA,** GOD OF THE SUN...
SOON I WILL BE **FREE,** FREE TO LIVE **FOREVER!**
Bwahahahahaha!!!!
DO YOU MIND? I HAVE TO READ THROUGH THE WHOLE THING TO FIND ALL THE INSTRUCTIONS.
ahem
O GREAT **RA,** GOD OF THE SUN...
WOOF WOOF
WHAT **NOW?**

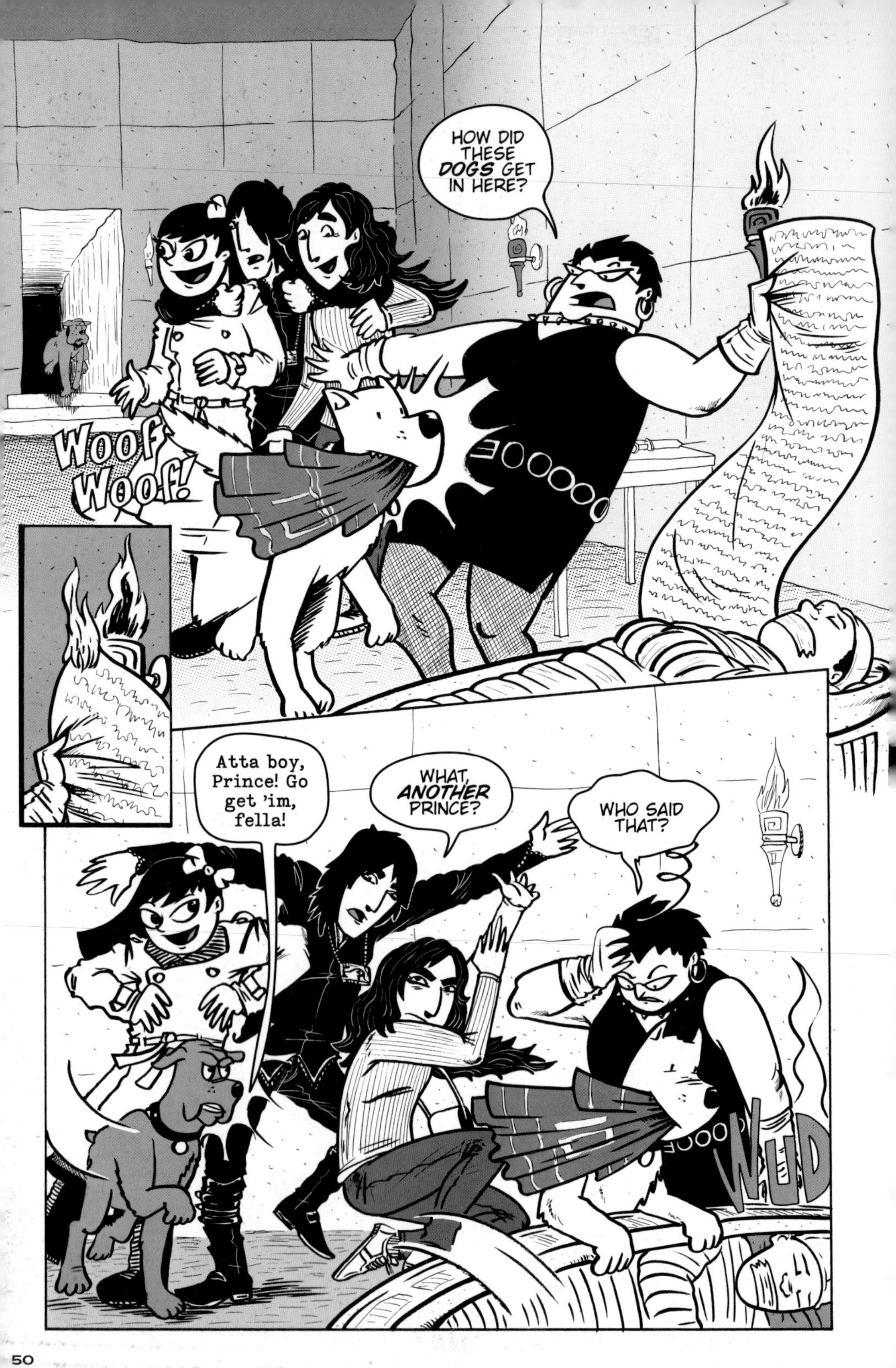
HOW DID THESE DOGS GET IN HERE?
WOOF WOOF!
Atta boy, Prince! Go get 'im, fella!
WHAT, ANOTHER PRINCE?
WHO SAID THAT?
WUD

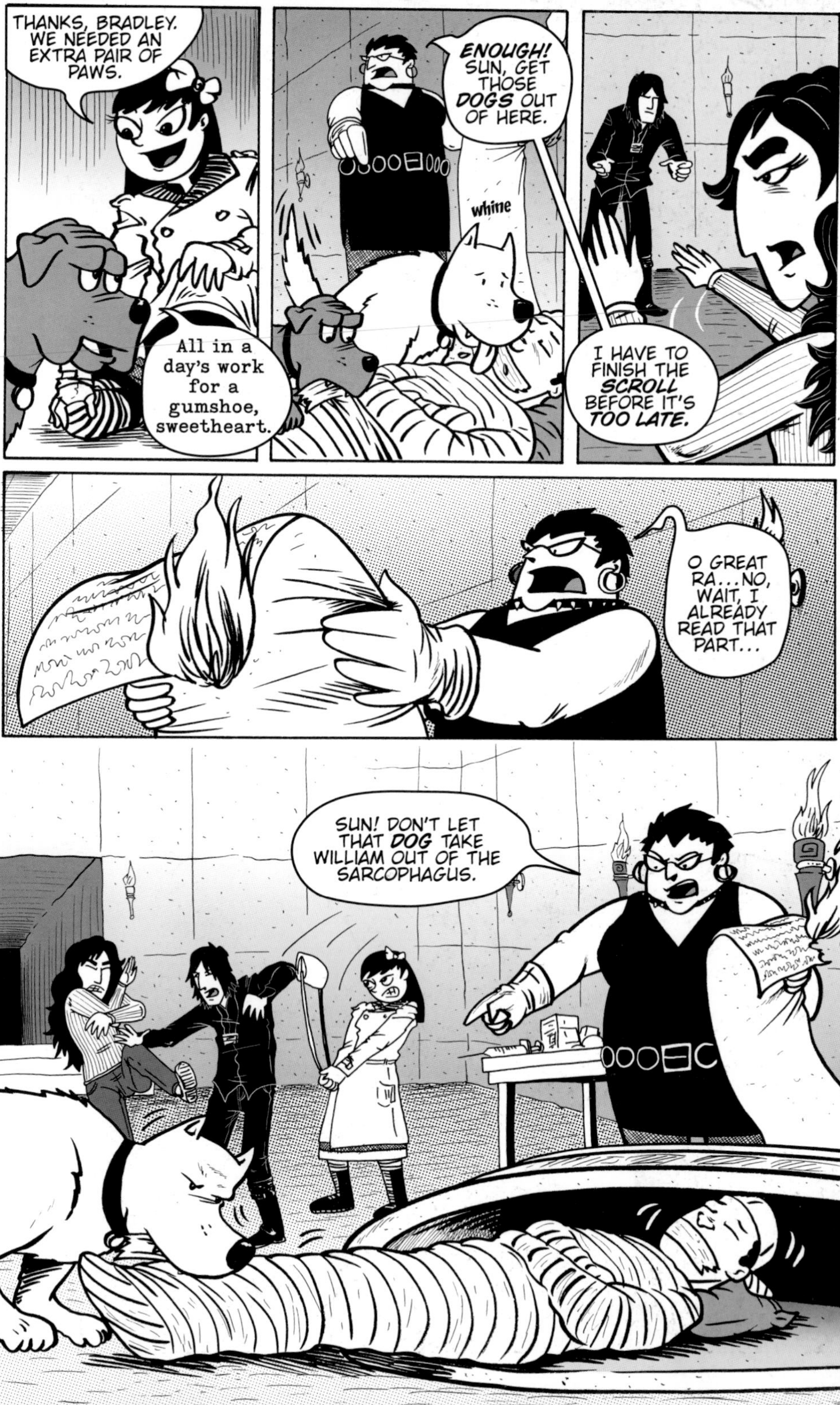

THANKS, BRADLEY. WE NEEDED AN EXTRA PAIR OF PAWS.
All in a day's work for a gumshoe, sweetheart.
ENOUGH! SUN, GET THOSE DOGS OUT OF HERE.
whine
I HAVE TO FINISH THE SCROLL BEFORE IT'S TOO LATE.
O GREAT RA...NO, WAIT, I ALREADY READ THAT PART...
SUN! DON'T LET THAT DOG TAKE WILLIAM OUT OF THE SARCOPHAGUS.

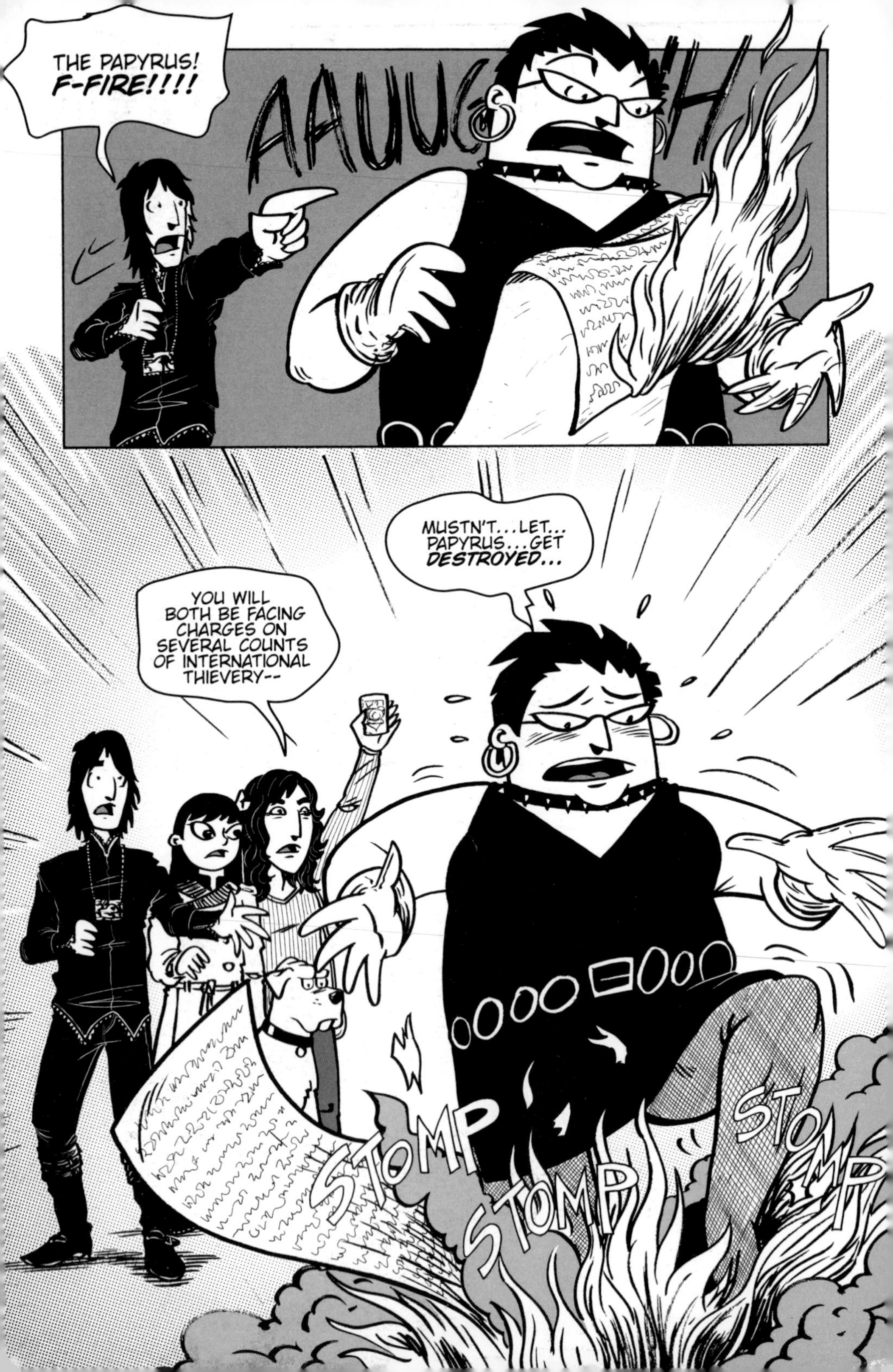
THE PAPYRUS! F-FIRE!!!!
AAUUGGHH!
MUSTN'T... LET... PAPYRUS... GET DESTROYED...
YOU WILL BOTH BE FACING CHARGES ON SEVERAL COUNTS OF INTERNATIONAL THIEVERY--
STOMP
STOMP
STOMP
STOMP

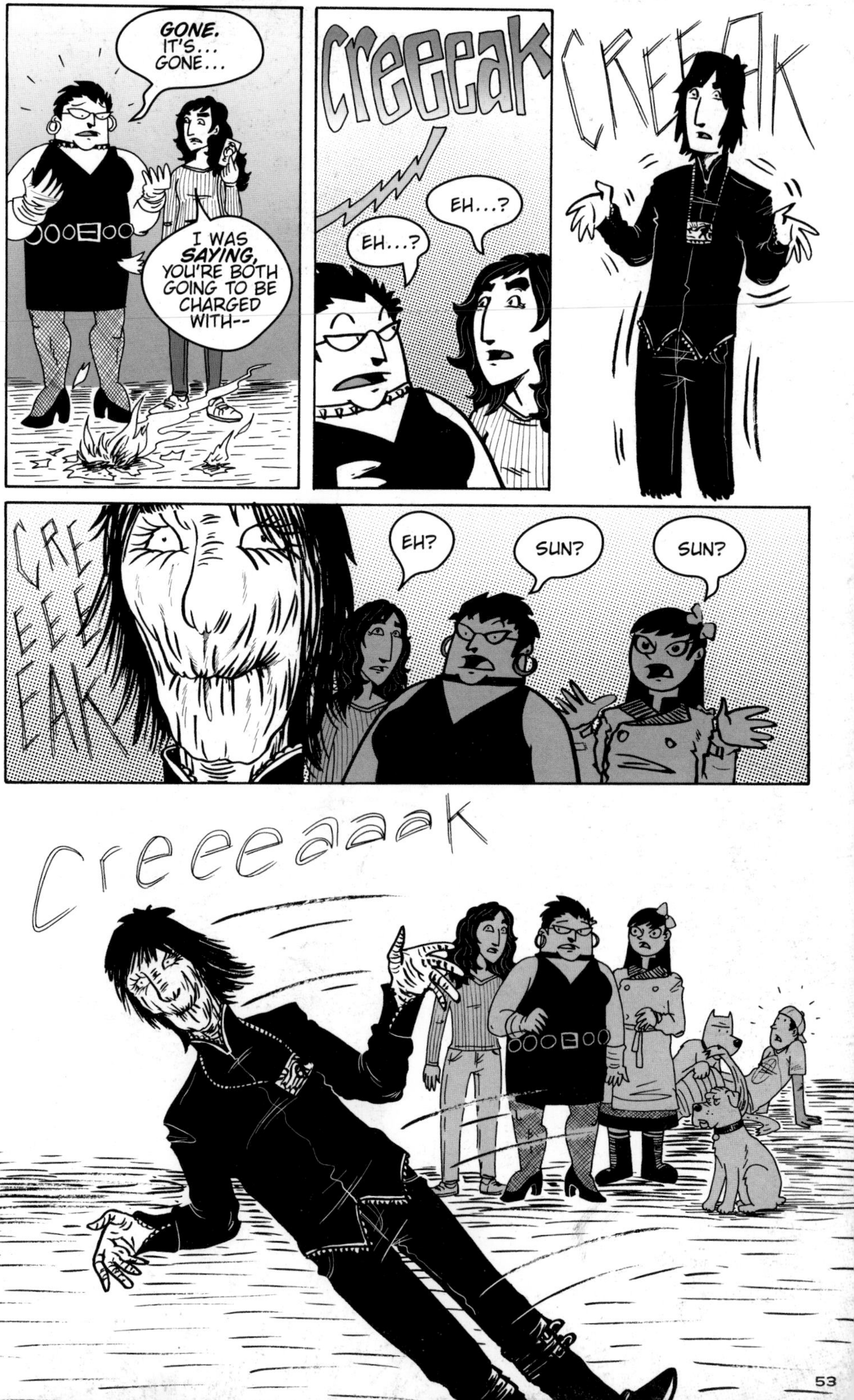
GONE. IT'S... GONE...
I WAS SAYING, YOU'RE BOTH GOING TO BE CHARGED WITH--
CREEEAK
EH...?
EH...?
CREEEAK
CREEEEEAK
EH?
SUN?
SUN?
Creeeaaak

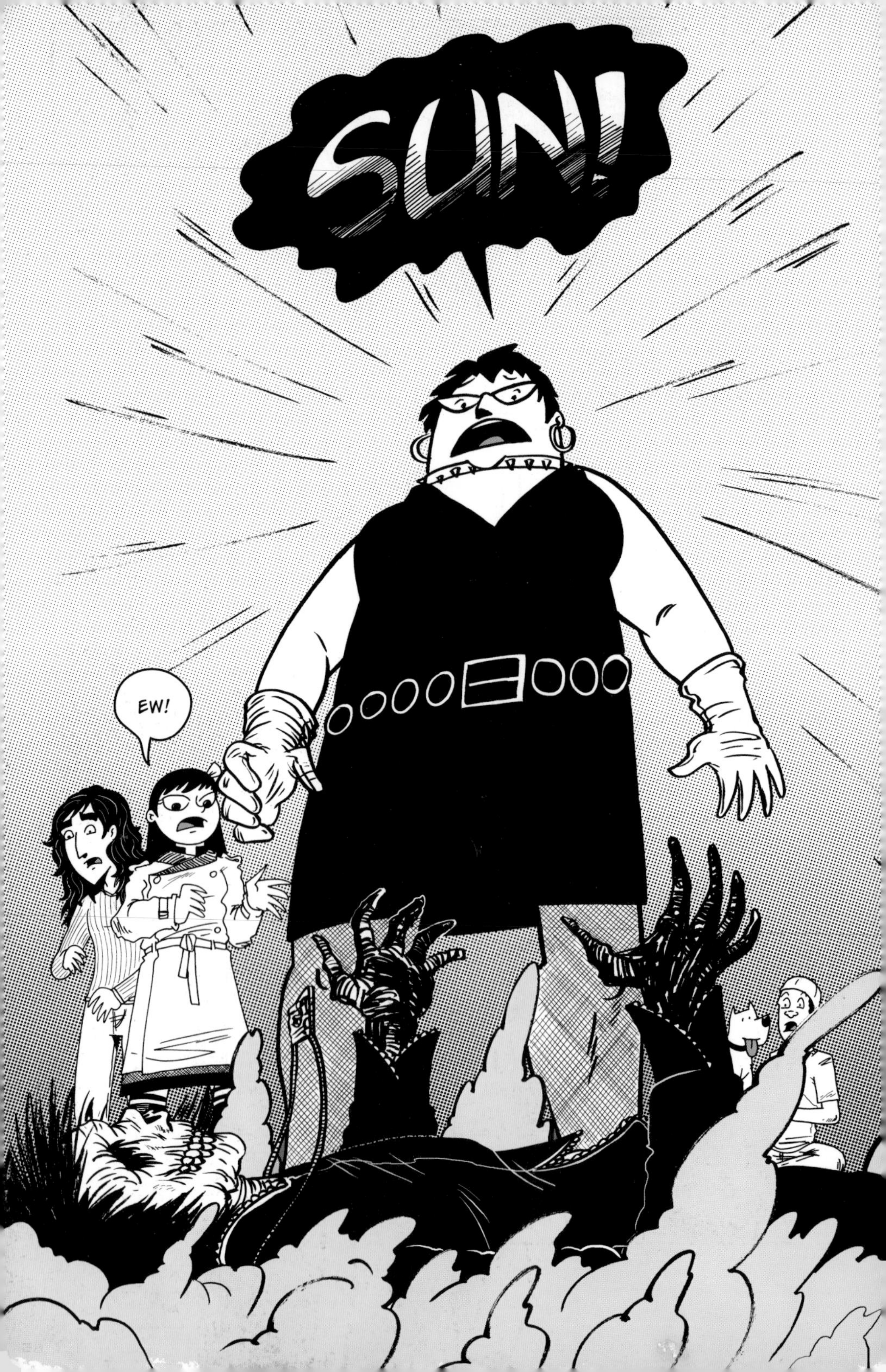
SUN!
EW!

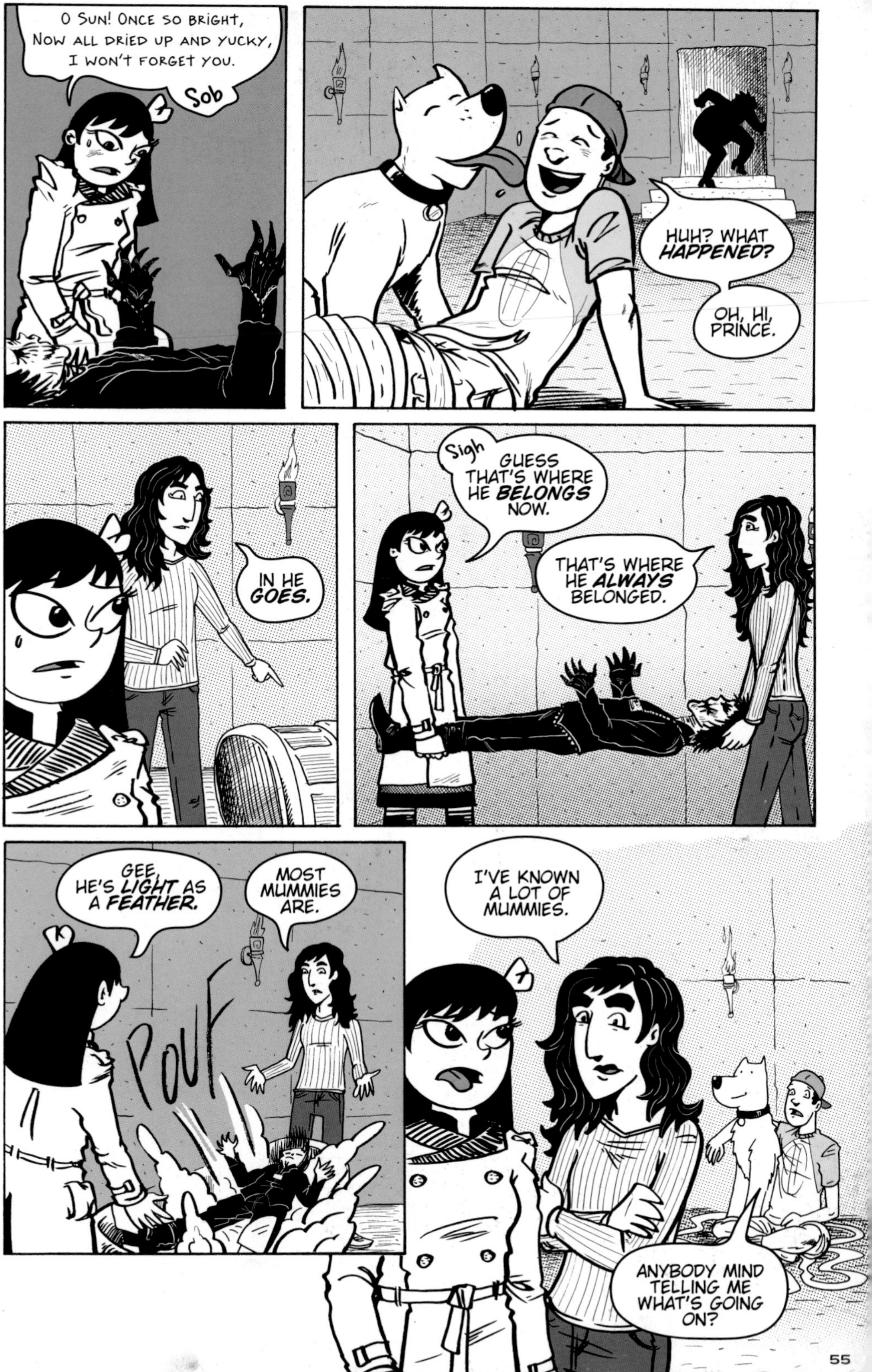
O SUN! ONCE SO BRIGHT, NOW ALL DRIED UP AND YUCKY, I WON'T FORGET YOU.
Sob
HUH? WHAT HAPPENED?
OH, HI, PRINCE.
IN HE GOES.
Sigh
GUESS THAT'S WHERE HE BELONGS NOW.
THAT'S WHERE HE ALWAYS BELONGED.
GEE, HE'S LIGHT AS A FEATHER.
MOST MUMMIES ARE.
POUF
I'VE KNOWN A LOT OF MUMMIES.
ANYBODY MIND TELLING ME WHAT'S GOING ON?

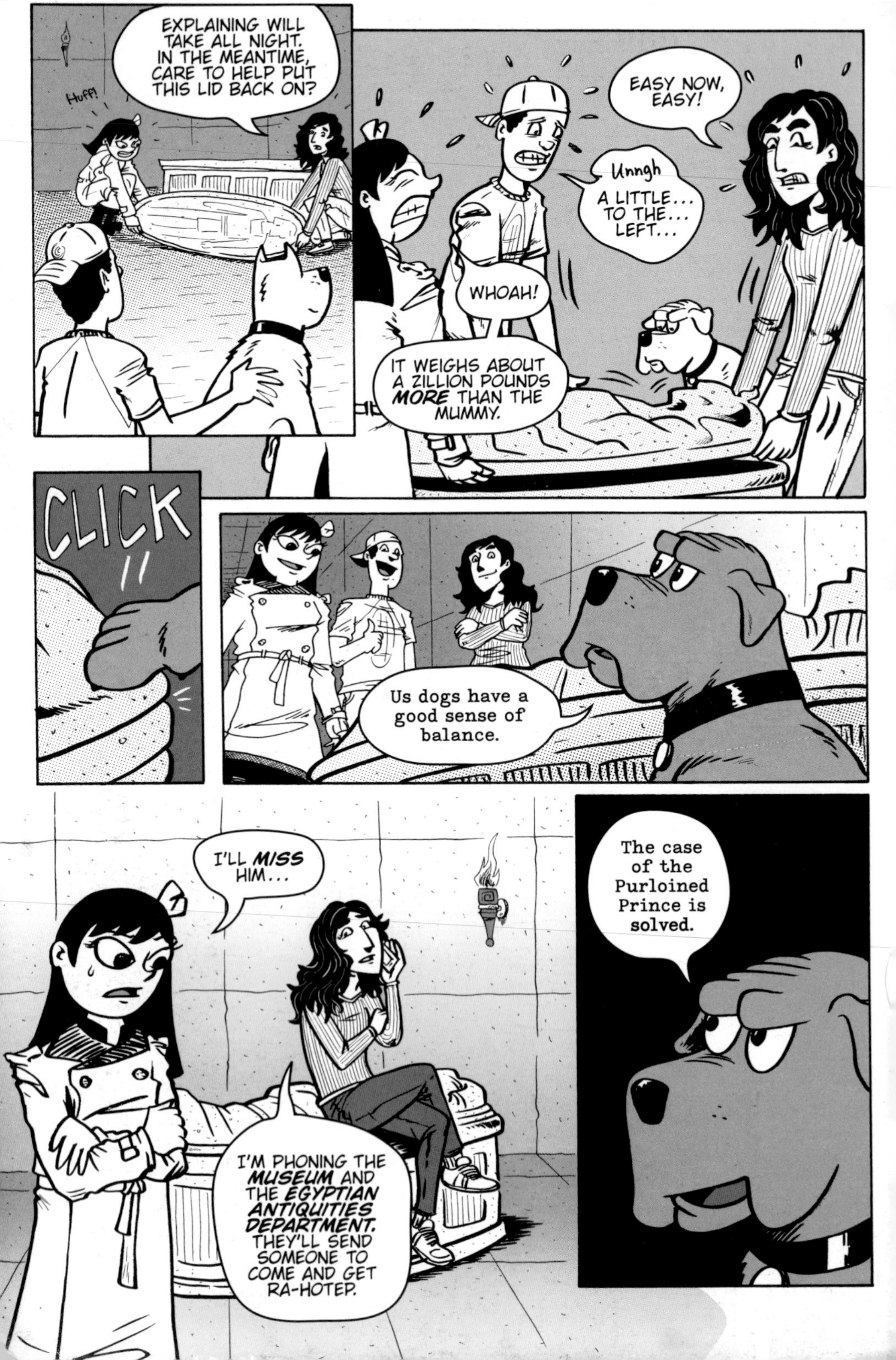
EXPLAINING WILL TAKE ALL NIGHT. IN THE MEANTIME, CARE TO HELP PUT THIS LID BACK ON?
Huff!
EASY NOW, EASY!
Unngh
A LITTLE... TO THE... LEFT...
WHOAH!
IT WEIGHS ABOUT A ZILLION POUNDS MORE THAN THE MUMMY.
CLICK
Us dogs have a good sense of balance.
I'LL MISS HIM...
I'M PHONING THE MUSEUM AND THE EGYPTIAN ANTIQUITIES DEPARTMENT. THEY'LL SEND SOMEONE TO COME AND GET RA-HOTEP.
The case of the Purloined Prince is solved.

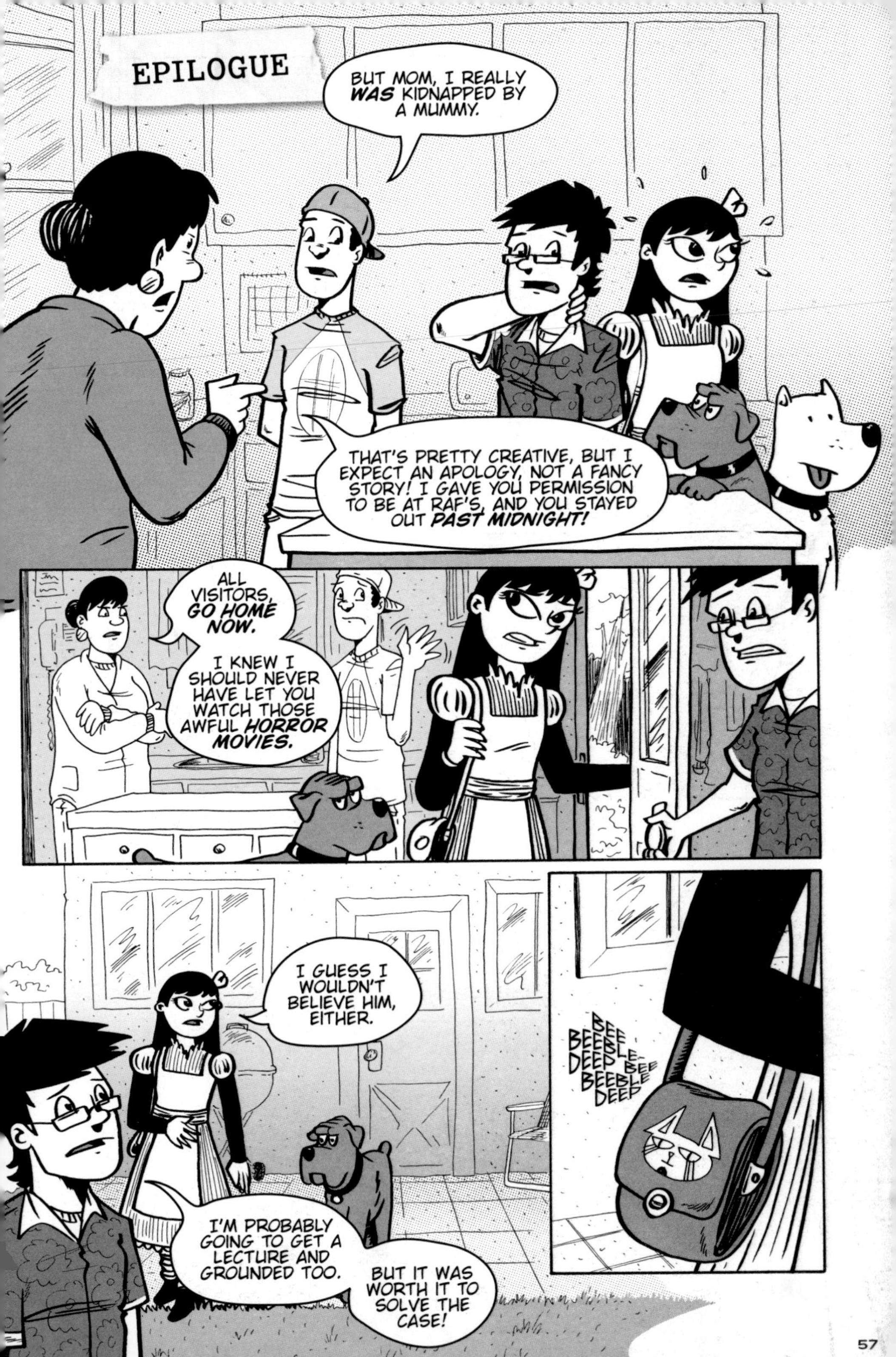
EPILOGUE
BUT MOM, I REALLY WAS KIDNAPPED BY A MUMMY.
THAT'S PRETTY CREATIVE, BUT I EXPECT AN APOLOGY, NOT A FANCY STORY! I GAVE YOU PERMISSION TO BE AT RAF'S, AND YOU STAYED OUT PAST MIDNIGHT!
ALL VISITORS, GO HOME NOW.
I KNEW I SHOULD NEVER HAVE LET YOU WATCH THOSE AWFUL HORROR MOVIES.
I GUESS I WOULDN'T BELIEVE HIM, EITHER.
I'M PROBABLY GOING TO GET A LECTURE AND GROUNDED TOO.
BUT IT WAS WORTH IT TO SOLVE THE CASE!
BEE BEEBLE-DEEP BEE BEEBLE DEEP

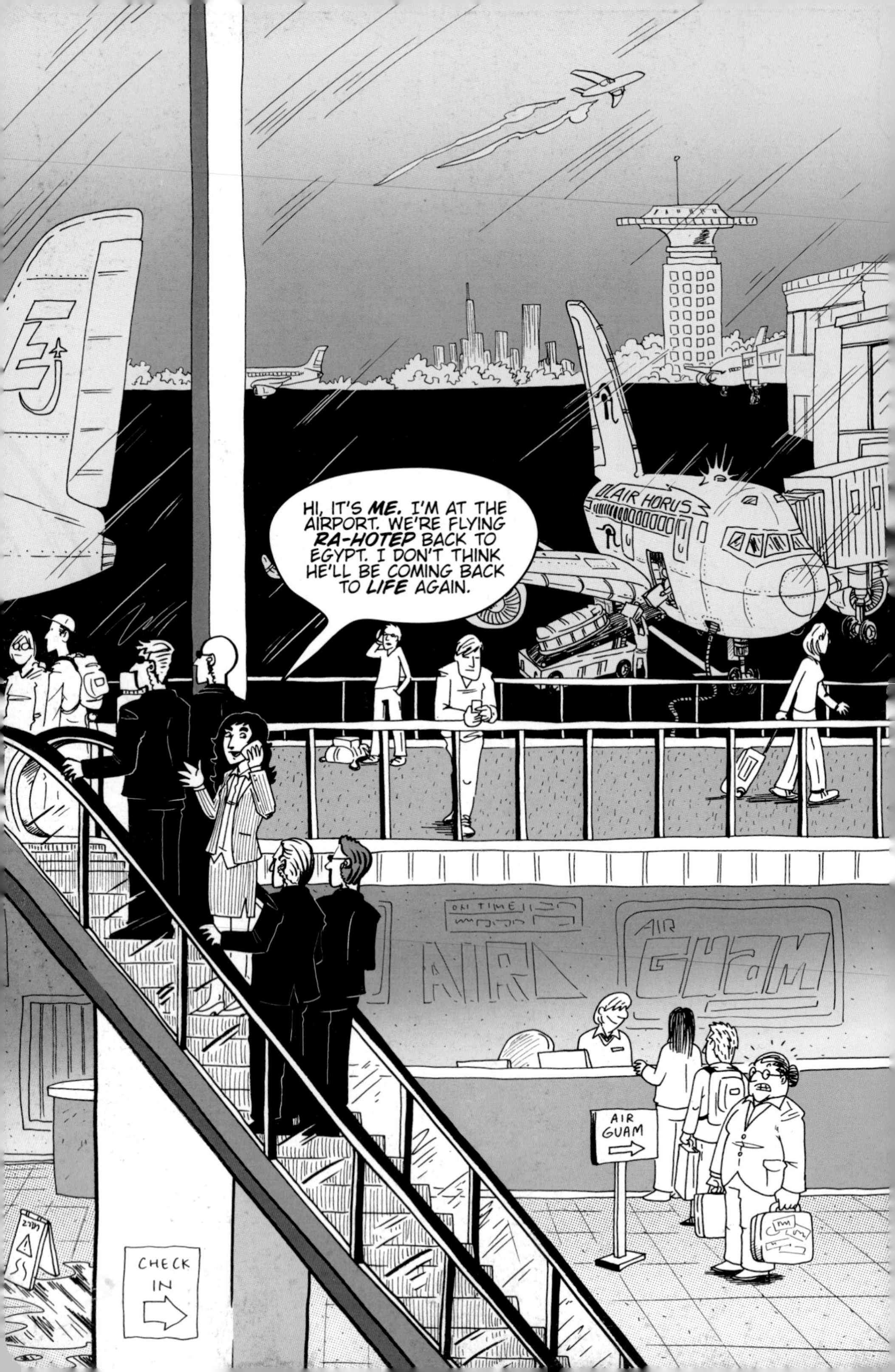
HI, IT'S ME. I'M AT THE AIRPORT. WE'RE FLYING RA-HOTEP BACK TO EGYPT. I DON'T THINK HE'LL BE COMING BACK TO LIFE AGAIN.
AIR HORUS
ON TIME
AIR
AIR GUAM
AIR GUAM
CHECK IN

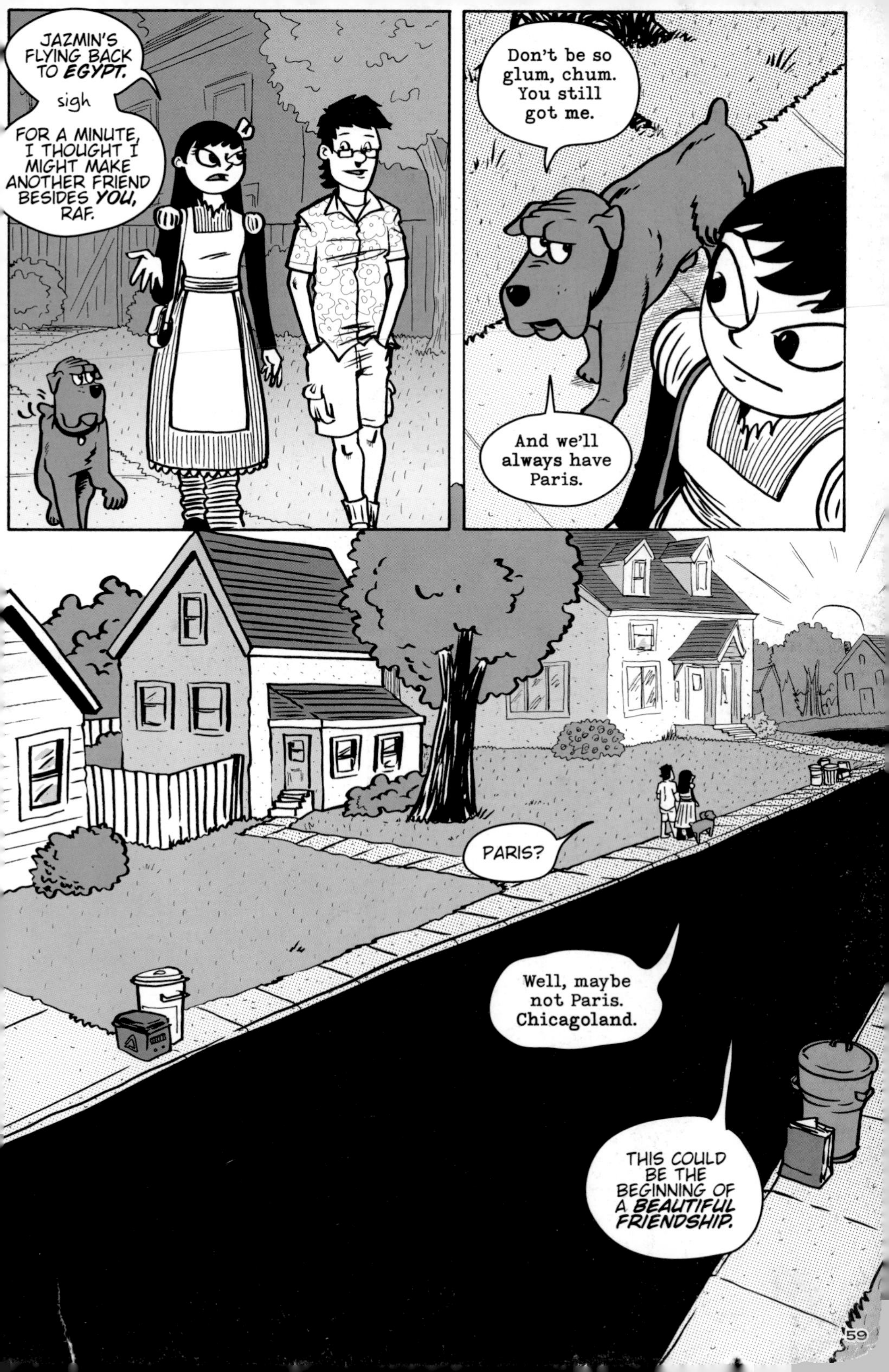

JAZMIN'S FLYING BACK TO *EGYPT.*
sigh
FOR A MINUTE, I THOUGHT I MIGHT MAKE ANOTHER FRIEND BESIDES *YOU,* RAF.
Don't be so glum, chum. You still got me.
And we'll always have Paris.
PARIS?
Well, maybe not Paris. Chicagoland.
THIS COULD BE THE BEGINNING OF A *BEAUTIFUL FRIENDSHIP.*

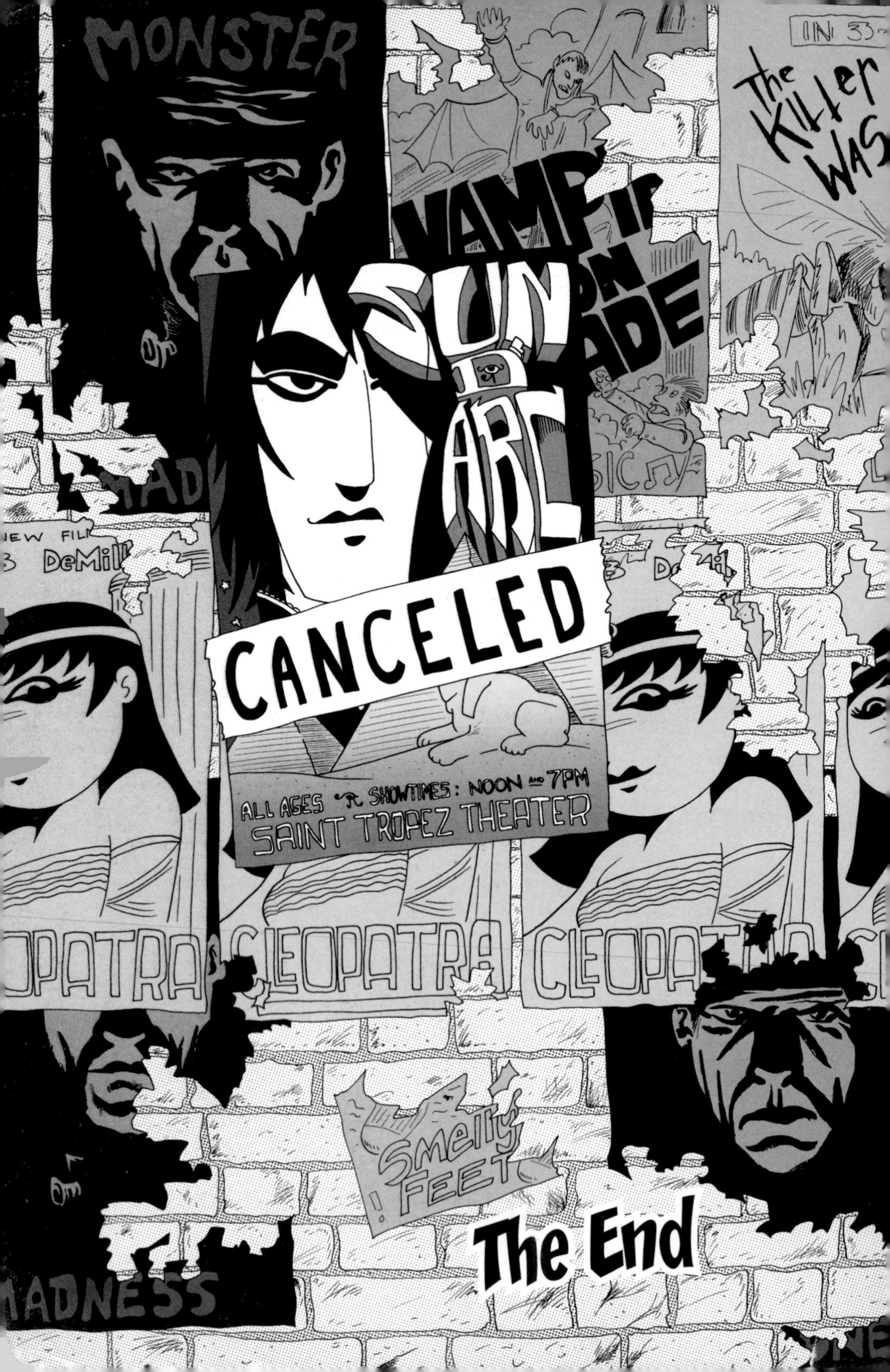

MONSTER
IN 33
The Killer WAS
CANCELED
ALL AGES
SHOWTIMES: NOON AND 7PM
SAINT TROPEZ THEATER
DeMill
CLEOPATRA
Smelly FEET
ADNESS
The End

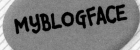

MYBLOGFACE

CHICAGOLAND DETECTIVE AGENCY

Our motto:
Stumped? Scared? Need help fast?
Chicagoland Detectives:
We can do the job!

The Chicagoland Detective Agency is here for you. We solve low crimes and misdemeanors, and we battle injustice. Don't be afraid to come in with your pets. We love animals.

InforFACEtion

Location: Behind the counter of Hernandez & Sons Pet Supplies

Hours: 9–5 during summer vacation. During the rest of the year, afterschool hours, except on weekends

Proprietor: Raf Hernandez (that's me) because it's my mom's store

Friendly FACErs

3 Friends

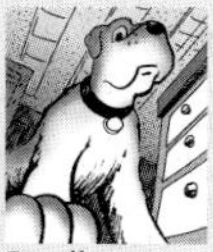

Bradley

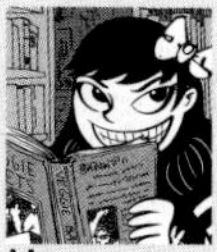

Megan Yamamura

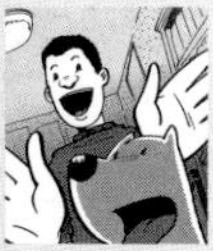

William Johnson

Meet the FACE

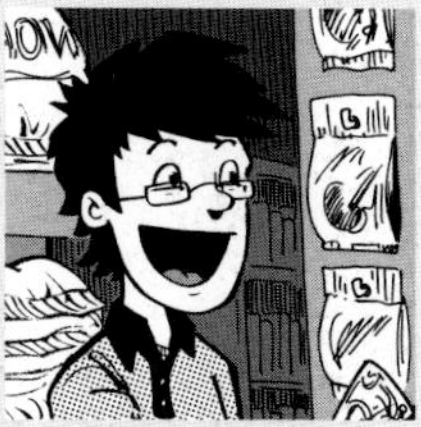

Raf Hernandez

Age: 12

Education: James A. Garfield Middle School

Chicagoland BLOG ENTRY #2 ⊠

LET'S TALK MUMMIES!

The Chicagoland Detective Agency just solved a big case that involved antiquities smuggling and Egyptology. The mummy of the teen king Sun D'Arc was a huge part of the case.

The Egyptians preserved the bodies of their dead so that the dead could enjoy an afterlife in the Heavenly Fields. This afterlife was supposed to be just like their life on Earth, only better. So the kings and queens and rich people were buried along with little statues of servants, who would continue to serve them in the afterlife. This worked out fine if you were royalty or nobility, but wasn't so hot for the servants, who just continued to be servants forever. So hardly a democracy, no. continue...

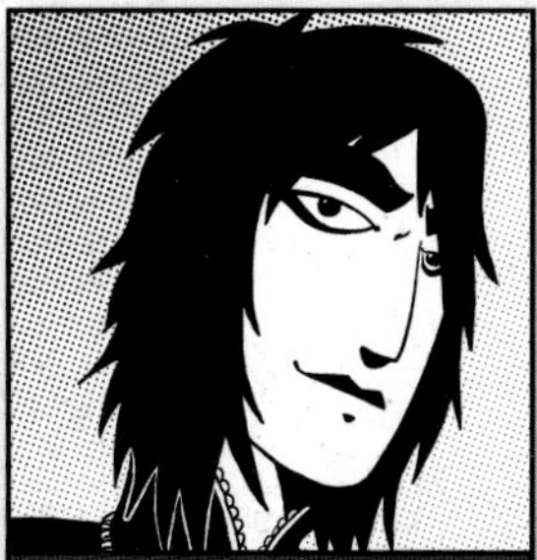

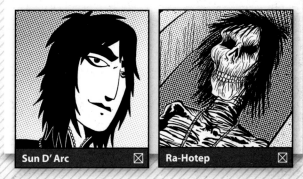

Sun D' Arc ⊠

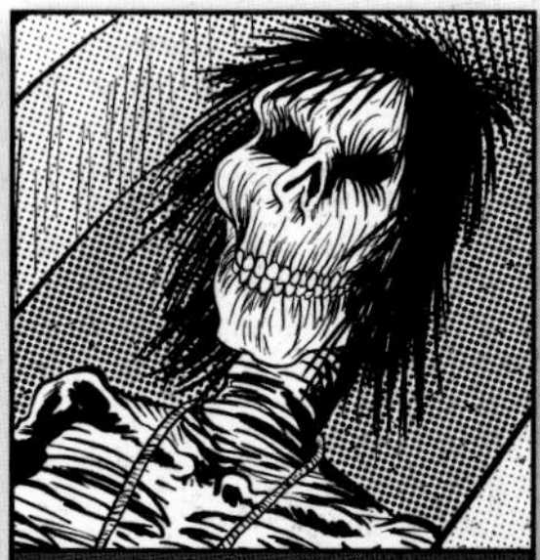

Ra-Hotep ⊠

Chicagoland BLOG ENTRY #2 continued

They say the goddess Isis invented mummification when she mummified the body of her husband, the god Osiris, after he was killed by his jealous brother Seth. Isis must have loved Osiris A LOT and also must have had a strong stomach, because the mummification process is pretty gross. Usually it was NOT performed by wives on their husbands, but was done by professional embalmers.

First, the embalmers pulled out the brains of the dead person through the nostrils. Then they cut open the body and removed the internal organs: the lungs, the liver, the kidneys, the intestines, and the heart. They soaked all those pieces in a kind of salt solution called natron for 40 days. After that, they wrapped up each organ like a little mummy and put it in its own little mummy case or jar.

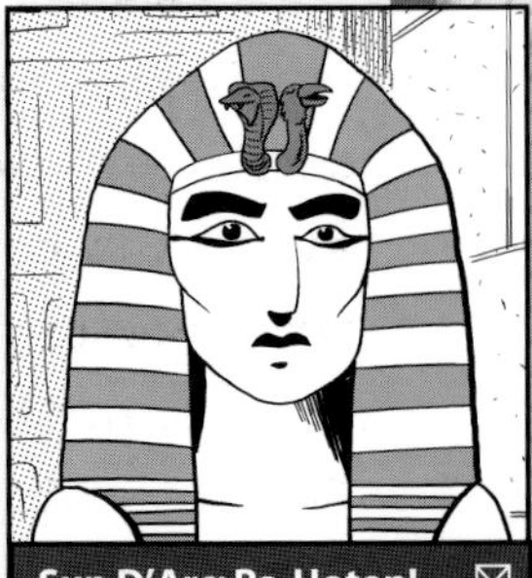

Sun D'Arc: Ra-Hotep!

Are you grossed out yet?

Meanwhile, the embalmers were doing the same thing with the body, soaking it in natron for 40 days until it was dehydrated, then stuffing it with linen and spices, and wrapping it up in more long strips of linen. During this time, professional mourners, hired for the job, would wander the streets shrieking, beating their breasts, pretending to pull out their hair, and pouring dust on their heads.

So maybe the mummies didn't wind up living again (except for some of them), but all that pulling out of brains and salting of livers turned out to be a good thing after all. Now scientists can examine 2,000-year-old mummies and find out all sorts of cool stuff about life in ancient Egypt. Such as what killed the famous teen king Tutankhamen, whose name means something like "the living image of the hidden sun god." Turns out the poor guy probably had all sorts of things wrong with him, including a cleft palate and a clubfoot, so he may have had to walk with a cane (he had a huge collection of them). But what killed him was likely malaria. Not murder, like some people used to think. It took a lot of detective work to find out all these things about someone who lived over 3,300 years ago.

Remember, the Chicagoland Detective Agency (chicagolanddetectiveagency.com) can find out all sorts of other cool stuff for you. You can find me behind the counter at Hernandez & Sons Pet Supplies weekdays after 3. We barter!

2 COMMENTS:

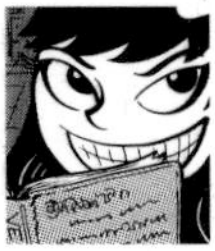

Megan Yamamura A word or two about the ancient Egyptians that my esteemed colleague missed: they wore AWESOME makeup! They practically invented eye makeup. In fact, they probably DID invent eye makeup. That black stuff they lined their eyes with is called kohl, and it helped prevent eye infections. As soon as my extremely conservative dad, who mistakenly thinks 13 is too young, lets me, I will get some modern eyeliner and make up my eyes exactly like they did and, in fact, the way I did in my past life when I was Nefertiti, queen of Egypt.

My dark eyes recall
Past life as Nefertiti,
I must wear kohl NOW!

September 25 at 1:15 PM

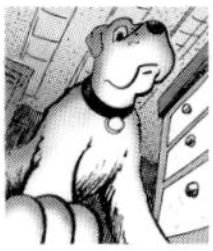

Bradley Personally, I think the ancient Egyptians were overrated. These guys worshipped—*are you ready?*—CATS! Cats were so important to them that when the family cat died, everybody would shave their eyebrows! They even turned their cats into little cat mummies!

But what about dogs? Did they worship dogs? When the faithful household doggie, man and woman's best friend, went to the Great Frisbee in the Sky, did they turn the little guy into a mummy? Did they shave their eyebrows? Not a chance!

Bunch of losers.

September 26 at 4:45 PM

ABOUT THE AUTHOR AND ILLUSTRATOR

TRINA ROBBINS, an Eisner Award and Harvey Award nominee, made a name for herself in the underground comix movement of the 1960s. She published the first all-woman comic book in the 1970s; published her first history of women cartoonists, *Women and the Comics*, in the 1980s; was an artist for the *Wonder Woman* comic book; and created the superhero series *Go Girl!* with artist Anne Timmons. And that's just a start—she has written biographies, other nonfiction, and way too many other books and comics for kids and adults to list, but you can check them out on her website at www.trinarobbins.com. She lives in San Francisco with her partner, comics artist Steve Leialoha.

TYLER PAGE is an Eisner Award-nominated illustrator and webcomic artist who has self-published four graphic novels, including *Nothing Better*, recipient of a Xeric Foundation Grant. His day job is director of Print Technology at the Minneapolis College of Art and Design, where he oversees the college's print-based facilities. He's been drawing his whole life, and sometime around middle school started making his own comics starring the family cat. He lives with wife Cori Doerrfeld, daughter Charlotte, and two crazy cats in Minneapolis, and his website lives at www.stylishvittles.com.

STUMPED? SCARED? NEED HELP FAST?

CHICAGOLAND DETECTIVE AGENCY CAN DO THE JOB.

NO CASE TOO WEIRD!

The word is out that Megan, Raf, and Raf's talking dog Bradley are the team to go to when even weirder things than usual start happening in Chicagoland. The Chicagoland Detective Agency takes danger in hand (and paw) to find a mysteriously missing puppy and an even more mysterious pack of dogs that only shows up once a month.

Bradley can tell from the start: this is more than a simple case of stray pets... and a whole lot more than a stray case of full-moon transmogrification! Can high tech and haikus save them all from the world's worst case of doggy breath?

The mystery will be chased down in...

CHICAGOLAND DETECTIVE AGENCY #3

NIGHT OF THE LIVING DOGS

BY TRINA ROBBINS

ILLUSTRATED BY TYLER PAGE